Rafat paused in his cleaning, stepped outside, and pulled out his golden fountain pen, a birthday present from his mother. That was the advantage to night cleaning. He could always stop to capture a couple of lines. He couldn't be certain, but it felt like his songs were getting stronger.

Night sky, tight sky
everything all right sky,
soon no moon,
babe, let's croon.

Maybe spoon? Both old-fashioned words—which his mom would appreciate, haha.

He was about to start another verse, but before he could write "Light sky," he saw a flash of something in his peripheral vision, something shining in the dusty moonlight.

"No!" he thought, turning to face the assailant, Rafat's pen extended like a weapon.

The knife cut into him before he could lunge. It struck again and again. The young man was dead before he hit the ground, notebook clenched in his hand. His cherished fountain pen rolled quietly away from his body, as steps retreated.

Mars Hill Murder

by

Mary Tolan

This is a work of fiction. Names, characters, places, and incidents are either the product of the author's imagination or are used fictitiously, and any resemblance to actual persons living or dead, business establishments, events, or locales, is entirely coincidental.

Mars Hill Murder

Contact Information: info@thewildrosepress.com

Cover Art by *Kim Mendoza*

The Wild Rose Press, Inc.
PO Box 708
Adams Basin, NY 14410-0708
Visit us at www.thewildrosepress.com

Publishing History
First Edition, 2023
Trade Paperback ISBN 978-1-5092-5177-3
Digital ISBN 978-1-5092-5178-0

Published in the United States of America

Dedication

To Larry and Sally Tolan, who loved to read—to themselves and to all six of us. And to my sons Tolan and Will, who make me laugh and boost me up.

Acknowledgements

While novels are usually written by one person, it's a fact that we isolated writer types do not create books in a bubble. Many people helped me with *Mars Hill Murde*r, which I wrote over a period of ten years. It took that long because of my "real" jobs—reporting and teaching.

I want to thank those who read drafts of this murder mystery including stellar writers in their own right: Mary Hays, Stephen Long, and Stephanie Innes, as well as readers Jenny Tolan, Antoinette Beiser, Mandy Metzger, Molly Brown, Tolan Thornton, Ellen and Michael Houser, and Peggy Daly. Professional writer and editor Tammy Greenwood read this when it was twice as long and half as good, and had the guts to tell me so.

When most of your siblings are writers, it's tough not to compete and compare. Yet Tom, Kathleen, Sandy, John, and Yam Tolan—four of them writers, and one a photographer/baker—have always been fired up for me regarding my writing dreams.

Patrice Horstman and Lulu Santamaria looked over the book contract, and only let me pay them with a dinner. That was a fun night! Writers Annette McGivney, Janna Jones, and Stephany Brown were always ready to talk writing. Tolan Thornton and Will Thornton gave me good ideas, plus pep talks.

My stellar editor Dianne Rich at The Wild Rose Press was the first person in nearly a decade of sending out queries to see the potential in *Mars Hill Murder*. During the editing process she made insightful suggestions and dead-on corrections, always with a warm message, even reminding me toward the end of the process to breathe—and tie my shoes.

During the Covid years while I finished this book, my friends Stephany Brown and Donn Johnson were my main pod pals and helped me stay at least somewhat sane.

For those of you who know Flagstaff, you'll notice that businesses have new names in these pages. This is for legal purposes, and not because I don't love you as you are.

Any errors are, of course, my own.

Prologue

Alejandra Lopez put extra effort into her polishing. She wanted to see the metal rails of the telescope platform shine. Some night, she hoped to come back to this amazing Flagstaff observatory as a visitor, no scrubbing involved, and see what the astronomers watched through the glass housed in this long metal tube. She had often gazed at the distant stars from her hometown in Mexico, but she had never seen the pinpoints of light up close. She guessed it was like looking at diamonds. Los diamantes del cielo.

She felt lucky her sister and brother-in-law had asked her to work tonight. After arriving from Mexico just the month before, she was ready to help out, and she wanted to show them that. She didn't plan on cleaning as a living in the United States, however. No, gracias*! She was a teacher by trade and hoped to continue that in the States if this* loco*, wealthy country let her stay. She figured there must be lots of American children who needed to learn Spanish. Meantime, she would do anything for her family.*

She and her sister had been close as girls, and when Feliciana left for America with Juan it had devastated Alejandra and their parents. She felt isolated without her best friend, but believed she was needed at home. Since then, both their mother and father had passed on, and now the sisters could be together again. She would get to know her nieces and nephews and start a new life. She crossed herself—quick but reverent. When her sister Feliciana caught the flu last month, Juan had asked Alejandra if she would fill in. Of course she would. Now she came up here a few nights a week.

Alejandra thought she heard something outside the telescope building. She stood up straight, cleaning rag in hand, listening to the night. She heard another train in the distance.

“Dios Mío*!” she whispered. She'd never been anywhere with as many trains as this place called Flagstaff, Arizona.*

She turned back to her cleaning, when a sharp, cool breeze crept up from behind. She turned around in time to see the big door had opened. She looked back into the shadows beside the door where the overhead light didn't reach.

“¡Hola! Quién es?”

Alejandra's screams were muffled by the sound of the freight train passing through Flagstaff, the engineer laying on the horn to keep wildlife and drunks off the tracks.

Alejandra Lopez took her last breath, imagining the glittering stars.

She didn't feel her body being stabbed again and again, or being dragged into the nearby woods, or the cold ground underneath her. She didn't see the dark sky of stars winking above her.

Footsteps hurried away, but she didn't hear them.

Chapter 1

Miles Harper left the newsroom and walked over to cover the protest at Wheeler Park. He looked over the gathering assembly in Flagstaff's small, downtown park that sat between the library and city hall.

About one hundred people stood in front of a temporary stage set up next to the dry Rio de Flag. The speaker, a young, fit Hispanic woman, spoke to the crowd, alternating between English and Spanish. The people had gathered to protest the Arizona law that cracked down on illegal immigration.

She called out, "*Si se puede*," and the crowd chanted the words back to her.

"Yes we can," she said, and they echoed her again.

"SB 1070 equals discrimination and racial profiling," the young woman said in Spanish and then English. The crowd booed and hissed.

"It means that white people can come and go as they please, but brown and black and red people can be stopped, even if they've lived here for generations."

Miles pulled his narrow reporter's notebook out of his back jeans pocket and began writing as fast as he could. He copied down the words of some of the placards the people held high.

"Does my face look like an alien?"

"Arrest me, not my friends!"

While most of the people at the rally did seem

upset, there was also a festive feel to the gathering, Miles thought. A mix of urgency and camaraderie.

Miles walked through the crowd of twenty-somethings, middle-aged, and old people, about two-thirds Hispanic and a third Anglos, with some Native Americans sprinkled throughout the crowd.

After jotting down some of the quotes from the speakers, Miles walked over to a group of counter-protesters, who were waving their own signs.

"Keep our boarder's safe," one read. *In need of some spellcheck*, Miles thought, then tried to pull his own prejudices in check. If he weren't a journalist, he'd probably be organizing gatherings like this, and arguing with this small group of counter-protesters. But, as a reporter, he knew he had to keep his neutral stance so he could tell a story to his readers through unbiased eyes.

He approached a woman dressed in red, white, and blue, who was deep in discussion with a couple others donning patriotic colors.

"Sorry to interrupt, ma'am. But can I ask a few questions?" Miles began. "I'm a reporter for the *Gazette*."

"I'm surprised you're even willing to talk to our side," the woman responded.

"Oooooh!" one of her group responded.

"Go get 'im, Jillie," another teased.

Her friends moved closer, and the woman faced Miles.

"What do you want to know then?"

"Just why you're here. I assume you're against the message of the main protesters."

"You can say that again," she said, nodding toward

the platform. “I don’t have anything against people coming to our country, but let’s keep it legal. None of this sneaking over the borders. That’s a crime.”

“It is,” Miles conceded. “What about those who are fleeing violence and gangs, and who say they want to help their children have better lives?”

“Oh, you’ve bought all that hook, line, and sinker, have you?”

“I’m just asking.”

“Well, then. I’m just answering. My great-great grandparents came over from Europe all those years ago, but they came into this country legally. You wouldn’t have found them sneaking over in the dark of night. They worked hard, all the next generations did, and to have that all exploded into smoke by illegal aliens, no thank you. It’s just not right.”

Miles noticed her contemporaries waving her over.

“Got one more minute?” he asked. “I’d like to get your name, and what you do for a living, all that. Do you live in Flagstaff?”

“Name’s Jillie—Jillian Carruthers. I’m a stay-at-home mom, and our ranch is about eighteen miles east of Flagstaff.”

“And the ranch is—”

“Gotta go now,” she said, walking away, but then turning back to him.

“Be sure to spell my name right. The media always gets it wrong. J-I-L-L-I-A-N C-A-R-R-U-T-H-E-R-S.” And she walked off.

“Will do,” Miles called to her back. He wondered how many times she had been interviewed, and for what.

About to leave the park, he noticed the woman

seemed to be arguing with a couple of men in her group. He walked back over to them.

"…not a good idea to talk to the press," a tall man was telling Jillian.

They stopped talking when he joined them.

"Something else?" Jillian asked.

"I wondered if anyone else wanted to talk to me for the story."

"I got nothing nice to say 'bout the illegals who sneak into our country and take away our jobs," said the extremely tall man in thick glasses wearing a John Deere ball cap.

"That's the truth," added another man, shorter, skinny, and with a couple days' growth of facial hair. "Bet you've never lost a job to no illegals."

"Yeah," agreed John Deere.

Jillian looked concerned, and Miles thought she might be worried they were taking it too far. He was wrong.

"Listen, Miles Harper. We don't begrudge anyone coming into our country. But as these guys said, Americans who work hard should not be undercut by aliens. They are lazier than we are. It's just their nature."

"It's from growing up in the warmer climates," John Deere said, nodding.

"Got it, thanks," Miles said, starting to turn away.

"So did you ever lose a job to anyone from outside?" asked the second man.

"Yeah, *did* you?" echoed John Deere.

"You're right, I didn't ever lose a job to someone new to this country, as far as I know," Miles said, choosing his words carefully. "So I don't know what you've been through. Either of you want to tell me your story?"

They all glanced at each other and shook their heads.

"I think you have enough from what we told you," Jillian said.

Miles wrote down the names of the two men and walked out of the park.

They had a point. Not about the laziness, of course, but about the fact that he, Miles, was lucky enough to never have been pushed out of work due to immigration. But it still riled him. He was glad they'd talked more to him, though, so he could create a balanced story. Let the readers decide. It was kind of a cop-out on his part but, hey, it wasn't like he was writing a think piece for *The Atlantic* or *Harper's*. He worked for a small daily paper, covering the news.

Walking into the *Gazette* office, he breathed in the smell of ink from the presses, body odors, and a dustiness that was probably an accumulation of the last few decades the newspaper had been in its downtown location. He loved it all. He pushed through the half door that swung open into reception and turned left into the newsroom.

"Got something good?" hollered Ruth Swanson, his editor, a five-foot-two, stout woman with spiked orange hair and matching lipstick, manicure, and shiny four-inch heels. Her voice seemed too low for her minute body. "You're pushing deadline here, so I hope you got a super interesting story."

"I'm on it, boss," he told her. "Give me a half hour."

"Make that twenty, Harper. We held a six-inch

hole for you."

"No way!" He was shocked. "This is a big story."

"For today, make it a little story," Ruth demanded. "You can fill in more online and for tomorrow's paper. I told you to get back here in under an hour."

Miles groaned internally, then sat down at his desk and powered up his computer. He knew he had pushed it by talking to the anti-protesters a second time. And deadlines were deadlines. But, still. Tell the whole story in six damn inches? Oh, well. He'd do his best.

The newsroom workstations were across from each other. In the large room, sets of four metal desks were pushed together, each arrangement forming a rectangle where three or four reporters or editors faced each other, with monitors at each desk. There was the news section, sports, features, and the editors. Because of recent cutbacks at the paper, however, about a quarter of the desks went unoccupied. Miles's desk, which faced away from the newsroom door, was one of the farthest from his editor's workplace.

He jumped into the story, telling the readers the background of Senate Bill 1070, the protesters against it, and those who were protesting the protesters. Six inches came and went, and he was just finishing at about twelve inches when Ruth called out to him again.

"Harper, it's time," she said simply.

He reread the copy, cut out four inches, made a few Associated Press corrections, and hit the "Send" button that would place it on Ruth's computer screen. The AP guidelines were grammar and spelling rules followed by newspapers across the country. They were picky, but for Miles they were great because it made grammar choices clear. Just take a peek at the AP Stylebook, the reporters' Bible, and you were good as gold. Or at least silver.

"Jesus, Miles, eight inches!" It was Ruth's turn to groan. But she was reading through it and nodding—always a good sign. He hoped there would be room on one of the jump pages to get it all in, condensed as it was.

Miles stood up, stretched tall, and walked out of the building for a breath of mountain air. He'd lived in Flagstaff for nearly five years this second time around, and still couldn't get enough of the air, the biking and running trails, the pace. He had discovered all this as a college freshman a dozen years ago and became hooked on the lifestyle. After graduating from the University of Northcentral Arizona—UNA—with a bachelor's in journalism, he returned to the Midwest where he'd grown up, to work at a weekly paper in Chicago, and later for a small daily in the suburbs.

But he found he missed the San Francisco Peaks, the blue, blue skies, and the simpler life. When a reporting slot opened up at the *Gazette,* he jumped on it. And never glanced back.

He'd been surprised how much he loved working in a small community, covering everything from local politics to small-town intrigue to firefighter-saves-kitten-in-tree stories.

Butch Patrick, one of the paper's ad reps, stuck his head out the front door.

"Dude, Ruthless needs to talk to you," he said, using the editor's nickname.

"Thanks, Butch." Miles pushed himself off the wall. "How's your morning goin'?"

"Another day, another half a dollar," Butch

answered, shrugging.

"Right? I hear ya," Miles responded as he often did to Butch and others at the paper. Most weren't happy with the pay and the hours, but for Miles, it had been as brilliant a change as the Arizona night sky.

They walked into the building together.

"You trying to get a beard going, dude?" Butch asked, smirking.

"Just haven't shaved this morning," Miles joked. His pitiful excuse of a beard was actually the splotchy result of a month's growth. But he had faith that it might turn into something decent—eventually.

"You rang?" he queried Ruth.

"Good stuff, Harper. Strong," said Ruth, nodding to her computer screen. "I made a couple of AP Style corrections and a suggestion on your lead. Take a look."

"Right."

Over her shoulder, Miles read through her changes and begrudgingly nodded. She'd made his lead less explosive yet more informative, but without changing the meaning. Basically, the story alerted the readers—or *audience* as it was called nowadays to take into account the multiple ways people were getting their news—that SB 1070 was controversial and had harsh critics as well as strong supporters. The state bill added onto the U.S. federal law that required adult immigrants to keep certificate of alien registration on their person at all times. Arizona's law said that law enforcement officers who made a "lawful stop, detention, or arrest" of a person, determine their immigration status. The state law also made it illegal for state or local officials to restrict their law officers from enforcing the federal laws.

Miles had explained that in one long paragraph, and Ruth had made it both shorter and clearer.

Damn, I should have caught those AP Style errors, he thought. *Next time.*

"Thanks, boss. Sorry about those mistakes."

"Now slap an update of the city parks story onto the website, and be sure to get both stories out into the virtual SM, too," she said referring to social media platforms.

Miles knew this was the new world of his chosen career. Write the story, post the story, tweet the story, Facebook and Instagram the story. He'd recently read a quote from a former publisher of the *New York Times*: "The important word in newspaper is not *paper* but *news.*" Point taken.

Miles finished sending both out into cyberspace, and returned to Ruth's desk, where she was reading his update.

"Good," she said in her gravelly voice. "Now, if I recall, you have two days off, so take them before I decide we need you to cover the Flagstaff Unified School District Board meeting."

"I'm outta here, boss."

"Ruth. The name's Ruth. I don't want to have to tell you that again."

"Got it. Sorry, Ruth. See ya then."

"You going anywhere? I'll need to be able to reach you."

"Camping and biking is all."

"Okay and, listen, the powers that be have made the decision to go to a morning paper early next year. We'll have a building-wide meeting next month to learn more about the details. But come the beginning of 2011, deadlines will be moving from late morning to the night before the paper comes out."

"That'll be an adjustment."

"It's the future, Harper. Actually, it's past time. We're the last damn evening paper in the state, and one of just a handful across the country. When I go to newspaper conferences, my counterparts just shake their heads when I tell them we're still an evening paper."

"I get that."

"And we're also going to talk about the new policy that says all reporters will keep up a blog—a professional one, of course. So think about how to write about your beat in a way that's different from just the reporting."

"Can't wait."

"I'm training a new assistant editor-slash-reporter while you're out. You'll meet her when you return. Now let me get going on these pages."

"Right. See ya, Ruth."

But she wasn't quite done with him.

"Oh, and I want to wish you luck."

"Luck?"

"With that emaciated mouse on your face," she said, leaning back in her chair, grinning.

"Hey!" he said, stroking his chin.

"Maybe in a month you'll have three damn patches instead of that miserable one," she said.

"I'll miss you, too," he shot back. Ruthless she was.

After glancing over the cascading piles of papers on his desk and promising himself he'd tackle them on his return, Miles shoved a couple of reporter's notebooks into his backpack and headed for the door.

While most reporters now used digital recorders or their new oh-so-smart phones to take notes at meetings and in interviews, Miles sat firmly in the school that used both. Of course, there was no substitute for the accuracy of a recorded quote, but the four-by-eight-inch spiral reporter's notebook, made to fit into a back pocket, never ran out of batteries. By using both, he could keep good eye contact, yet jot down highlights of his interview to come back to when writing the story.

He walked outside to his bike. He stroked his no-longer bare chin and smiled. Maybe he'd never shave again. It wasn't that bad, was it? He felt it added depth of character to his unexceptional face, dishwater blond hair, and hazel eyes.

Two days off from the *Gazette.* What was he going to do with his time? He hopped on his trusty one-speed and cruised downtown. He would check out the new location of Caboose Coffee, his favorite coffee shop. When he did have the occasional day off, he often hung out here or at Lacy's, Flagstaff's first real coffee house, south of the tracks and close to UNA, Miles's alma mater. Last week, Caboose Coffee moved one block north of its original location into a larger space across from the county courthouse. After getting a mocha, he'd ride home and call his mom, and then have the rest of the day to himself. He was freeeee.

Today, life's so good, I may just have to yodel, he thought.

And so he did.

Chapter 2

Maddy Sullivan stood outside of the Mountain Motel, her backpack and suitcases on the driveway, holding Daisy's red leash. She raised a hand toward the departing taxi, as if the driver were some long-lost pal.

"Are we a bit desperate for friends, girl?"

Her fuzzy black pal thumped a white-tipped tail and gazed up at Maddy. The dog smiled through her underbite.

"Well, it's been a long, long week—okay, a long few years," Maddy said. She shrugged on her backpack, grabbed the suitcase handles, and gently pulled the leash. The motel's lights were on, yet even in the daylight Maddy saw that only the MO and MO glowed, absent their UNTAIN and TEL.

"Let's go check in at the MOMO," Maddy said.

Pushing open a heavy glass door, she saw a slight man behind the counter. He was stubbing out a cigarette and waving smoke away, as if Maddy and Daisy were the tobacco police. He looked up, smiling through pale teeth.

"May I help you?" he asked in a quiet voice.

"My name is Maddy Sullivan. I called ahead for a room?"

"Oh, yes, Miss Sullivan. We have it all ready for you. My name is Karan Vohra, and I am the proprietor."

Except for a bit of lingering cigarette smoke, the lobby was bright, clean, and inviting.

"May I?" Karan asked, stepping out from behind the counter and offering Daisy a heart-shaped dog treat. Daisy sat and accepted the heart. And then, instantly and deeply, Maddy knew they had landed in the right place. Flagstaff had been a guess, a shot in the dark, without much time to plan. She swallowed and took a big breath.

"Everything okay, Miss Sullivan?" Karan asked, watching her closely.

"Oh, yes, sorry. Just got distracted for a moment."

"Very good," he said, walking back behind the counter and pushing some papers toward her. "Please sign there, and initial there and there. And here is your key. You are on the second—top—floor in the back. It is near a staircase that takes you down to the wooded area for you and—your dog is?"

"Daisy."

"It's close to a trail for walking Daisy, and yet away from the street, so it will not be too noisy—though Flagstaff does have many trains traveling through on a daily basis."

"Sounds perfect," Maddy said, and meant it.

"And how long do you plan on staying with us, Miss Sullivan?"

"Oh, Maddy is fine. Let me see. I am really not sure of, um, of my circumstances. May I leave it open-ended for a bit? Maybe a month while I look for more permanent housing?"

"A month would be wonderful, Miss Sull—Miss Maddy," he said, smiling. "All we ask is that you give us forty-eight hours' notice before leaving. Does that suit you?"

"Yes, Mr. Vohra, that suits me."

"Karan, if you please."

Just then the bell over the front door tinkled, and a tall boy and smaller girl walked in.

They both went to Karan and kissed him on his cheek.

"Please say hello to our guest Miss Maddy," he told them. "Miss Maddy, meet my children, Tanak and Amita."

The three exchanged greetings, and Karan turned to his son.

"Tanak, would you please carry Miss Maddy's suitcases to Room 207? And, Miss Maddy, would you like Amita to help you with your backpack?"

Maddy looked at the shy girl who was now kneeling down, nose to nose with Daisy.

"I will get the backpack, but perhaps you could take Daisy for me, Amita?"

The girl smiled widely, and Maddy told the kids she would be right up. After they left, she turned to their father. She did not want to draw attention to herself, but something had to be said.

"Yes?" Karan said.

"Um, someone might—well, I want to be sure that, let's say, if someone were to call to find out if I was staying here, that you would, um, not give out that information," she said.

"I understand, Miss Maddy. We do not give any information out on our guests unless the guest explicitly tells us to take a message from someone. So if you're looking for a bit of privacy, the Mountain Motel is the place for you."

Maddy felt tears pricking her eyes. She blinked them away.

"That's it, Mr. Vohra—Karan. I am just looking for some privacy. Some down time." She liked the sound of that.

She wrapped her fingers around the room key and turned toward the door.

"Thank you so much."

"Wonderful to have you with us," he said.

Maddy walked outside and up the stairs to meet the children and the dog.

They dropped off her things in the room, but Maddy barely looked at it because she was desperate for a cup of coffee. She headed back downstairs with Daisy and the siblings and asked them about coffee shops in town.

"Are you driving or walking, Miss Maddy?" Tanak asked.

She told him she was walking but needed some exercise so did not mind a bit of a distance.

"Caboose Coffee or Lacy's," Amita said.

"Yes. But let's send her to Caboose Coffee, so they will not have to cross Route 66 and the train tracks," Tanak said, and his sister nodded.

They gave her directions, ending with battling descriptions of one of the downtown buildings on her route.

"Go past the old Federal Building," Tanak began. "It's made of cream-colored bricks and tan stones—"

"Not tan, silly. Pink!" Amita cut in.

"Tan!"

"You know why he wants them to be tan, right, Miss Maddy?" the girl asked.

Maddy shook her head.

"Tanak's nickname is Tan."

Maddy smiled. She promised them she would weigh in on the color debate when she next saw them.

She headed west on Route 66, Google-mapping the destination into her brand-new iPhone. Why had she waited so long to get a smart phone? Still, everything she'd done over the last three years was a mystery to her now. Who had she become? What had she lost?

She'd get a cup of coffee, walk around town, and call her old friend Belinda, who last Maddy heard was living in northern California. She hoped her pal would find it in her heart to answer—and forgive.

Looking north as she walked, Maddy could see mountains in the distance that shone green and gold. On her brief stroll downtown, three trains rumbled by, two headed east and one west.

"My God," she said to Daisy, seeing what Karan meant. "What is it with trains in this town?"

Could a person ever get used to the constant noise of the heavy train cars rumbling over the tracks? On just one of the trains, she lost count at eighty-seven cars, many of them closed containers, some with holes for animals to breathe, and several carrying shiny new cars and pickups. Then here came another one from the other direction. More pickups. Wow. She was officially Out West.

Maddy zipped up her blue fuzzy against the gusting wind, glad she'd worn jeans and running shoes. She flashed on the strapless dresses and lacy undergarments Arthur used to buy her and urge her to try on for his pleasure, and suddenly felt truly liberated. She'd wear whatever the hell she wanted from now on.

Dress up, if she liked. Dress way down if that was her mood.

She shook the man out of her head—hard—as she turned north on San Francisco Street. A mix of bars, Mexican, vegetarian, and Thai restaurants advertised their food, as well as a couple of Native American art stores, outdoor shops, a bike shop, and bookstore. Many of the stores had dog water bowls on the sidewalks. Daisy slurped from one outside the bike shop, and Maddy felt grateful and content. And then they passed it: The controversial Federal Building. Maddy smiled. To her, it looked tan in a certain light, but pink from another angle.

She liked those children. They seemed happy and fun, plus close. That all seemed possible for Maddy all of a sudden, too. She would let go of the pain and the fear.

A half block north of the Federal Building was the impressive county courthouse—red stones, and a tall clock tower with four faces. The three sides Maddy could see, though, each showed different times. Eight, eleven, and five. Maddy checked her phone. It was nearly two.

Daisy's ears perked up, and soon Maddy heard a strange sound. Sounded like a yodel, of all things. The yodel grew louder, and then a green blur of a bicycle raced by, brakes screaming as it barely made the turn into Caboose Coffee, directly across from the courthouse.

The Von Trapp family of Flagstaff?

Maddy hummed "My Favorite Things" and crossed the street, her mind calling up kittens, ponies, and Austrian raindrops.

Chapter 3

An eastbound bus pulled into Flagstaff Greyhound station in the wee hours of the morning, passengers waking from the wheeze of the brakes. Some rubbed their eyes, many peered out the windows, and a lucky few went back to sleep, destinations still distant. A handful of travelers got up and began collecting their things from the overhead compartments.

A few single men looking for work, a Spanish-speaking family with orange jack-o-lantern plastic bags for suitcases, a half dozen college kids returning to town after a long weekend in Los Angeles. A little boy held his sister's hand as he jumped down the bus stairs, a red cape flowing behind him. She smiled at him, despite being tired from the trip. A man in a white hooded sweatshirt wiped the sleep from his eyes and stepped off the bus. A teenager clicked his braces' rubber bands with his tongue, a habit he couldn't break, or didn't want to.

The bus driver sighed, ready for a couple of days off, relieved to be back in Flag. It would be good to clean up the bus for the next driver and go home. His wife would just be waking up, and he could have a decent breakfast with her and the kids. Maybe a snuggle after the kids were off to school. A guy could hope.

Outside, the passengers who stepped down the stairs were hit with the contrasting smells of sharp versus sickening sweet—ponderosa pine trees and baking dog food. It was too dark to see the dog food plant, but it was out there somewhere. A train whistled.

Chapter 4

Maddy looped Daisy's leash through the bike rack against which the green bike was leaning, patted her furry friend, and went inside. The line of customers seemed to include a few businesspeople, but also those whom Maddy guessed were students or tourists dressed as casually as she.

The yodeler stood a couple of people ahead of her. He looked like a college kid, with the requisite bike bag slung across his shoulders, blond hair curling on his neck. He turned around and she saw the old-fashioned wire-rimmed glasses as well as some unruly chin whiskers. He gave her a lopsided grin and turned back to the counter as he reached the front of the line

Maddy glanced out the door at Daisy. Tail wagging, the dog was surrounded by three small girls and a mom, who drew them into the coffee shop.

"Can we take the doggy home, Mommy?" asked the smallest girl.

"It belongs to someone," the oldest girl responded, though also looking longingly back at Daisy, whose tail was still wagging.

"Your sister's right, Lily. Now who wants a hot cocoa with whipped cream?"

"Me!" They responded in unison, and the dognapping was forgotten.

Then Maddy was at the counter. She ordered a

twelve-ounce, two-shot latte.

"One medium Train Track," called out the barista, wearing an Arizona Diamondbacks kerchief over his Afro. "Anything to eat?"

Maddy looked at the offerings behind the glass. "Let me try a lemon scone."

"Good choice," he assured her. "Next!"

After getting the scone plus the "Train Track" latte and picking up a weekly newspaper, Maddy walked back out to the patio, where she found Von Trapp rubbing Daisy's ears. Daisy was leaning into the guy. But when Maddy came out, Daisy jumped up, her entire backside wagging madly.

"And just when I thought I'd made my new best friend," the guy said. "She's a bit fickle, I see."

"We go back a way," Maddy said. "Plus, I have a scone."

"Right? There's that," he said, again with the lopsided grin.

She untied the leash and walked with Daisy over to a small table shaded by locust trees. The young man plopped himself down at the next table.

"How do you like the new location?" he asked.

"New location?"

"Caboose Coffee. You know, it used to be a block south of here, right next to Phyllis's shop? This is my first visit to the new space."

"I did not know all that. I never went to the old place," Maddy said.

"Really? Are you a Lacy's fan then?"

Maddy hesitated, kicking herself for not really figuring out what she would say to strangers about her life and the move. She had not had time to think anything through, except the leaving part. Not that Arthur would ever find her through some random college student, but still. He had a way of getting what he wanted—especially when it came to what he thought he owned. Or who.

"Lacy's, is that a store?" she asked. "And who is Phyllis?"

"You *are* new to town. No, our Lacy's is another coffee shop—all vegetarian, and it was the first real coffee house in Flagstaff. A real classic with customers that range from construction crews to professors and students to old-school hippies and tourists."

"So why are you not hanging out there between classes?"

"I'm not a professor."

"I thought you were a student," she said. Though now, in the sunlight, she saw he looked older than her first estimate. Not thrillingly handsome by any means, but not bad looking either.

"Right, right. That's been a while," he said, laughing, apparently assuming she was joking. The guy's entire face lit up when he smiled. He stuck out his hand. "Miles Harper. And Phyllis owns Autumn Moon, next door to where Caboose Coffee used to be. She makes potions and tinctures, sells beautiful Native art." He took a breath. "So what brings you to our fair town?"

Maddy took a bite of scone and broke off a piece for Daisy. It was a bit dryer than she liked, but the flavor was a wonderful mix of lemon tart and sugar sweetness. Stalling, she took a sip.

"Oh my goodness, that's wonderful," she said.

"They make a good cup," he said, taking a slurp.

Maddy could smell the chocolate wafting. He looked at her, waiting for an answer.

"I moved from back east," she said, working to keep her voice neutral. Wisconsin was not exactly the East Coast but *was* east of Arizona. "I have heard about Flagstaff for years and decided to come check it out for myself."

Miles took another big breath, ready for more questioning, but Maddy stopped him.

"Listen, it is nice to meet you and all, but I was really hoping to just maybe sit with my coffee and the newspaper. And be quiet."

"Oh, right. Sorry about that. Didn't mean to interrupt your day," he said, barreling on. "*Flagstaff Living*. Right. I work at the *Daily Gazette*—the same company that owns *Living*. It was an independent paper until we bought it out a few years ago. It used to have more news, then it went to entertainment, and now it's mostly music. Good stories, though."

Maddy made a point of opening up the paper.

"Oh, that's a good article," he said, looking over her shoulder.

"Miles, uh, listen. I am about to take Daisy for another walk but would like to sit here for a bit before I do that."

"Sure, sure. I get it," he said, turning away.

Maddy read the paper as she enjoyed her hot drink, glancing over at Miles once to see him stretched out with his eyes closed, soaking in the sunshine. He was actually handsome when his face was at peace. He opened his eyes and looked directly at her.

"Jeez, can't a guy get some privacy around here?"

"I just do not want you getting sunburned." She

attempted a joke. A joke! It had been a long while.

"Good point." Miles dove back into conversation. "You know recent research shows that most sun blocks aren't good for you? So you have to decide if you want to A, Absorb chemicals or B, Get sunburned and perhaps get skin cancer."

"Mmm."

Miles took the hint, stood, and stretched. He held out his hand to Daisy, who lifted a paw for a shake, and then to Maddy, who took it briefly.

"Good to meet you, ladies. Miles Harper at your service. And you are?"

"This is Daisy, and I am Madeline."

"I hope to see you both again, Daisy and Madeline."

"Okay, Miles. Have a good day."

He continued standing there, though.

"Hey, you could put her in your car and then shoot a movie and call it—wait for it—'Driving Miss Daisy.' " He guffawed loudly, and Maddy found herself joining in. "Seriously, though, if you're gonna be in town for a while, I'm always lookin' for hiking buddies. I can show you two some good trails."

"Thanks, Miles," she said, wishing he would just get on his bike and yodel away.

He handed her a business card, issued an exaggerated bow, and threw a leg over his bike. Finally, he rode off.

"Odd guy," Maddy murmured.

Daisy wagged her tail as she watched the bike disappear.

"Hey, you never wagged that way for Arthur," Maddy said.

Maddy tucked Miles's card into her back pocket, took several more minutes with her coffee and the newspaper, and then stood. She walked back through the downtown toward the MoMo. She put some quarters into a newspaper machine and pulled out the *Gazette,* folding it in half around the weekly paper. If, like most papers these days, the classifieds were thin, she'd go onto Craigslist Flagstaff, if there was a local Craigslist, and start looking. For jobs, and a place to live. She could not take a job where Arthur could trace her through the Internet. She thought again of calling Belinda, but realized she was not quite ready, not quite brave enough.

"So I am a chicken," she said to nobody.

Daisy trotted along, refusing comment.

Chapter 5

Miles unlocked the door to his apartment and carried his road bike inside, leaning it up against the bookshelf, next to his orange mountain bike. He hung his helmet over the handlebars. A guy could never have enough bikes, was his philosophy. The books on his shelves included *Astronomy Today, The Second Long Walk: The Navajo-Hopi Land Dispute, The Bean Trees,* and several Tony Hillerman mysteries, which he normally devoured in a day or two. He loved Hillerman's books, full as they were of Arizona and New Mexico scenes, most of them set on Indian reservations. The main characters were all natives, too.

He slipped off his messenger bag and dropped it lightly onto the couch. He was tempted to drop himself there, too, but wanted to get a real ride in before evening. In his small but functional kitchen, he started making a breakfasty lunch. He broke three eggs into a ceramic bowl. As he whisked them, he kept seeing the woman and her dog in his mind's eye. Madeline. Now that was an old-fashioned name. He noticed she hadn't told him her last name. She had blue eyes, he thought, or maybe green? There was a dark smudge under one of them. She had a warm smile but seemed reserved. At least with him. Then again, he'd been a real pest, and she probably thought he was some slime bucket trying to hit on her. Oh, God. He hoped he'd see her again and make amends. But how? He *did* want to get to know her. At least the dog Daisy was friendly. He'd also noticed the lack of wedding ring, though a pale band of skin on her left ring finger indicated there may have been one until recently. Hmm. He shoulda been a detective.

He sautéed onions, garlic, and red bell peppers and, when they were nearly translucent, he scraped them into a smaller bowl and poured the eggs into a hot, buttered skillet. As the eggs cooked, he popped a couple of slices of sourdough into the toaster and quartered an avocado. He filled a cone with Caboose Coffee Mountain Rim grounds and poured hot water for another coffee. When it was all done, he took his plate and cup out to the tiny backyard, plopped down a folding chair, and dug in.

At the first bite, he nearly moaned. He wondered if he might be a bit odd. None of the guys at work talked about cooking, not to mention the color of the sky or the sweet smell of the ponderosa pines. Oh, well. He couldn't change himself at this point.

After finishing his meal, he pushed away his plate and opened Hillerman's *Shape Shifter,* reading while he sipped his coffee. But he could not concentrate. He kept thinking about Madeline. She was beautiful, sure. But there was also something about her reserve, her obvious love for her dog, her smile.

If they were characters in a Hillerman mystery novel, what would Navajo cop Joe Leaphorn say? Or Jim Chee?

The phone rang, and he remembered he had planned to call his mom.

"Hi, Mom. I was about to call you."

“Beat you to it, sweetheart. How is your day going?”

“Good. I’ve got two days off of work—the first long break in probably half a year.”

“Good for you. That place works you too hard.”

“You know I love it.”

“Well, that’s what matters, of course.”

“How about you, Mom? What have you been up to?”

“Oh, let me see. I did my yoga class this morning and just got home from book club. We read, oh what was the title? A tough read, all about the illegal immigration issue, and how some people want to keep new people out of this country, even if the immigrants are fleeing violence and/or poverty. It’s crazy, the women I’ve known forever and whose grandparents came fresh off the boat from somewhere not all that long ago, who now say everyone else should stay away.”

“Some people just want to close the doors behind them.”

“So true, Miles. And so sad.”

“I covered a protest this morning, set up by people supporting immigrants, but there were others there calling them horrible names.”

“Just awful. Anyway, tomorrow I’m going over to your Aunt Jeanie’s, so I know I’ll have a wonderful meal and good conversation.”

“Say hi for me, will you?”

“Of course. You know she has a sweet spot for you in her heart.”

“It’s mutual,” Miles said, and then blurted, “I met someone!”

"You did? Good for you. Who is she? How long have you been dating?"

"Well, I just met her. I mean *just.* As in today at a coffee shop, ha! Her name is Madeline, and she has a dog Daisy, who seemed more interested in me than her human was."

"Oh, a dog is good. Well, if she has any sense, she'll see you're a catch, honey. Smart and sensitive and handsome."

"Okay, Mom. Okay."

"Well, I know I'm biased, but still. When do you see her again?"

"That's just it. I'm not sure if I ever will."

"Well, Flagstaff's a small place. I'm sure you will. Just keep going for coffee."

"That's my plan. Anyway, I should get going. I want to take a ride before dark."

"All right. Take care and talk soon."

"See ya later, Mom."

The only son of a widow, Miles stayed in touch with his mother often. His younger sister lived in D.C. and was incredibly busy pursuing her career as a lawyer, and their older sister had died in a car crash a decade ago. A drunk driver had slammed into their dad's car as he drove her to a dance rehearsal one night. They were both killed instantly. For a while it was unclear how the now-tiny family would survive, but over the years they had, each in their own way.

His mother had kept busier than ever, his sister Carla had thrown herself into school and work like a mad woman, and still did the same. Miles had cried himself to sleep every night—for years. He was unfocused and smoked too much pot, until he discovered journalism at the UNA student newspaper. That had saved him.

When he'd learned of the opening at the *Gazette*, he'd hesitated because he'd been working in Chicago, not far from his mother. But she was incensed when he told her he might not apply for the job. She knew how much he loved Flagstaff.

"Miles, you cannot put your life on hold because of your *mother,*" she had told him. "I'd never forgive myself. Plus, I loved visiting you at college. I'll hop on the train and come see you."

He had agreed, made the move, and they saw each other a couple times a year in Chicago or Flagstaff or someplace new. Still, why had he announced to her that he'd met this woman, Madeline? Maybe he was *too* close to his mom, considering his age.

He shook off his concern though, knowing they both appreciated their friendship since Miles had become an adult. He hoped that down the road he and his little sister would become good pals, too.

Now he slathered sunblock onto his arms and face—and mini-beard. He filled his water bottle, put on his helmet, and wheeled his mountain bike out the door.

Chapter 6

Maddy unlocked her motel room with the key attached to a bright blue plastic mountain range. The MoMo apparently did not believe in key cards. She liked that.

The room was perfect. A half-fridge, sink, and warm yellow walls welcomed her. A low counter divided all that from an overstuffed chair and a double bed. A small kitchen table and two chairs were arranged under a window. Because her room was at the end of the outdoor hallway, she would not need to worry about people passing by all night.

She poured dog food into Daisy's bowl and got out a plate for the to-go Thai curry she had bought on the way back to the MoMo. She poured bubbly water into a glass and sat at the table. It was delicious, the curry spicy but not killer hot, and Maddy realized how hungry she was. She had not expected great Thai food in a little Western town.

After washing up, she checked her watch. Seven thirty. Still a little early to get ready for bed. Or was it? At least it was dark outside. She happily pulled out of her suitcase the cotton nightgown Arthur had hated ("not sexy enough for that bad bod, darling"), laid it on the bed, and curled her legs under herself on the easy chair.

She looked through the classifieds in the *Gazette*,

but, as she had feared, they were on the *way* light side. She fired up her new laptop, the one she purchased for cash just last week—could it be only days ago that she had run for it? She shook the memories away.

Happy to discover there was a Craigslist Flagstaff, she clicked on jobs and read through what her new home had to offer. She knew she could probably get some kind of job at designing ads at a business or government office, but she had to find a job that did not leave a digital record for anyone to discover. Or rather, one specific someone.

Maybe she should try something entirely new, like become a forest service fire fighter. Not the right season though. And not that she really wanted to do that. A park ranger? But she really did not want to go back to school.

Become a Viral blogger read one ad.

"Whatever that means," she said.

Daisy thumped her tail in encouragement.

Romance novelists wanted.

"Definitely not up for that."

Dog walker, part-time.

"I would never, girl," she told Daisy. "You are the only dog I will ever walk."

Thump, thump, thump.

Grant writer, experienced only.

How hard could that be? Still, she had no experience.

Editor/visual designer needed for local food-movement newsletter.

She clicked on the link: *Food interest a plus, strong design experience a must.*

Well, Maddy was no foodie, but she liked food.

Who did not like food? And she did have a ton of design work under her Midwestern belt. She wrote down the contact info and read a few more ads. That was it in any jobs she was qualified for. Dang, thin pickings. But maybe there would be more jobs listed in the *Gazette's* Sunday paper.

After jotting down a few more names and numbers, she checked her email. Nothing noteworthy, mostly those annoying automatic Facebook messages, which she began deleting. Suddenly, she could barely breathe. A private FB message from Arthur. "Maddy, you belong to me."

She slammed shut her laptop before reading or deleting it. Her heart crashed against her ribs, palms suddenly damp, bile rising in her throat. She rushed into the bathroom and vomited. Afterward, she brushed her teeth twice, filled a glass with tap water, and rinsed her mouth over and over again.

How did this man, just a man, have so much power over her emotions? Where once he pulled her in like a strong magnet, now it was as if he was repelled from her by an opposing magnetic force. She sank into the chair, Daisy resting her head on her lap. She petted the dog blindly, breathing in and out, in and out, envisioning a yellow light over her head and then surrounding her. Just like the therapist had told her in Wisconsin, she could still her breathing and still her emotions. She would not think about the person she married, and instead try to figure out how he had such an effect on her. But not now.

"Let's hit the hay, girl."

It was eight thirty. She considered that not too early to go to bed in this new life. After all, she had lived through a very long day, a long week, okay, a long few years. She swapped her jeans and sweater for the blue and white flowered nightie she had worn before Arthur Dempster. The life that had included her friends, her work—and her self-esteem.

She scrubbed her face, brushed her teeth, and looked at herself in the mirror. Of mostly Irish descent with a touch of Hispanic from generations ago, Maddy had ink-black hair, a constellation of freckles across her nose, forehead, and cheeks, green-blue eyes depending upon the light, and a 31-year-old body that was pretty nice, she would have to say. What with running, swimming and, lately, yoga. She could hardly wait to hit the trails with Daisy tomorrow.

She tried but was unable to keep her eyes off the blue bruises on her neck, under her left eye, and, pushing her sleeves up, on her upper arms.

"You look just fine, woman," she counseled her reflection. "In a week or two, those will have faded, and you will be deep into your new, wonderful life."

She took a huge breath and let it out slowly.

"You will never let this happen again. Never."

Maddy slipped into bed and turned off the pine-tree-shaped bedside lamp. The MoMo knew how to decorate a room, all right. She felt strangely at home here. She pulled the curtains open and looked out at the night.

"Would you look at those stars, girl," she said to Daisy, who obliged by hopping up beside her. The dog circled twice and then flopped down, resting her chin on Maddy's chest.

Outside, a not-so-distant train whistled. She focused on the Western October sky and refused to reflect on the worst mistake she had made in her entire life.

Finally, she slept.

Chapter 7

Arthur Dempster hit redial for what must have been the hundredth time. He could not reach his damn wife. Driving home from his solo hunting trip—out of season but nobody had discovered him—he felt his frustration mounting. *Where the hell* was *she? Why was she not picking up?* She knew he was headed home today. A spasm of anger shot through his entire body.

He thought he had whipped her into shape. Apparently not. He did not want to break her into pieces, not really. Just convince her—any way necessary—that this was her life now, he was her life now, and it was a good one. He pushed redial.

His wife's cell phone, on silent mode, lit up in a Milwaukee landfill site. The phone's light blinked on and off, on and off, buried deep under a pile of stink.

Chapter 8

Miles slid down the mountainside, wildly grasping for something, anything, to stop his fall. His hands grabbed cool air.

After hiking up Mount Elden for two hours, he'd scrambled on his hands and knees with two hundred feet to go to keep his balance as the wind whipped around him. But he hadn't kept his balance, and now his stomach scraped along the rocks, as gravity pulled him toward the edge. He finally stopped the fall by rolling explosively to his side to avoid falling off the side of the mountain.

He sat up now, unable to avoid thinking about how close he'd come to going over the edge. He'd nearly become a statistic for the Coconino County Sheriff's Search and Rescue. That would have been embarrassing at best, deadly at worst. He sat up carefully, struggling to catch his breath and balance. The air was thin up here, some 9,000 feet above sea level. He took a long swig from his metal water bottle on which a sticker read, "My Other Vehicle is a Bike." He had crossed out "Other" and inserted "Only." He was proud of the fact that he owned two bikes—sometimes three—and no car or truck.

He ran his fingers over his right ribs, feeling where they'd been pounded by the rocks and stones. They didn't feel broken. He'd busted ribs previously during a bike accident and, damn, those hurt like hell—a knife piercing your lungs. This was more like a bruising, though one that hurt something terrible.

Now, strangely, he found himself flashing on that woman Madeline. Not in any kind of mystical way ("Your face came to me as I rolled facedown off the mountain," ha!). More like how embarrassed he'd be if she'd learned Search and Rescue had to drag him off the mountain at their own peril. He didn't even want to think about the ribbing he would have received from Sgt. Luis Ortega, his former college roommate and now a Flagstaff police detective.

Still, why even consider how some random woman might think of him? Well, she didn't feel random to him—though he knew he was being ridiculous. They'd only met once, for God's sake.

He would not mention the near accident to his mom, who worried too much about him as it was. He slapped at his pockets and searched his daypack for his cell phone so he could take a few pictures of the incredible view and send them to her. But his phone was nowhere to be found. Had it slid away from him over the edge?

He crawled away from the steep drop, then carefully stood. It got extremely windy up here, but the gusts were not crazy strong at the moment. He looked out over Flagstaff. To the east he could see one train headed away and one coming into town, and he could barely hear the trains whistling. He spotted the sparkling white dome, the university's sports arena—and, to the north, the green-brown of the largest contiguous ponderosa pine forest in the world. The San Francisco Peaks were just past their golden glory of turning autumn aspen leaves, though he could see a few remaining sparkles of yellow. On Mount Elden itself, though, more fire-blackened trees stood than the live ones.

Miles stretched tall. Youch! He sat back down gingerly and pulled from his pack a snack of an apple and trail mix—including dark chocolate chips—munching for several minutes while he looked up at the clouds gathering over the Peaks. It was October and late for the regular autumn monsoon season, but this year the stormy season had started late and lasted longer than normal. He needed to be off the mountain before a storm rolled in this evening, or he'd be soaked by the rain.

He began hiking down, thinking about Mount Elden as he carefully chose his steps. The mountain was more than 2,000 feet in elevation above Flagstaff, which was at approximately 7,000 feet. The mountain, geologically a lava dome, had burned in one of those Southwest forest fires that were on the rise. The Radio Fire had swept through the mountain in 1977, more than three decades ago. Caused by an abandoned campfire, the flames spread quickly and offered a kind of mesmerizing town activity—as entire neighborhoods watched its progression from the safety of their backyards or on lawn chairs in the streets. On the thirtieth anniversary of the fire, Miles had interviewed local residents who had witnessed the blaze. They told him about the Forest Service using B-17 and B-24 bombers to subdue the flames. And how, through binoculars, many people of Flagstaff had watched huge pine trees explode in the heat, the flaming shards rocketing up and igniting more trees, over and over. In the end, 4,600 acres were lost, and the mountain still did not look anything like the green San Francisco Peaks on the north side of town—which also had a larger than safe buildup of dangerous fuels. Today's forest fires were much bigger, gobbling up tens of thousands of acres in a day, due to decades of lack of thinning—years of the Forest Service believing in Smokey the Bear's slogan of "Only YOU can prevent Forest Fires." This "no-burning is good policy" philosophy had caused the fuel loads that were now ravaging the West. And, too late, Forest Service folks were eating their words now, as they fought to get control of the dry, dense forests.

Miles remembered that nobody had been criminally charged in that 1970's fire. These days, though, people were fined and even jailed for careless neglect that caused fires, and especially for premeditated arson.

Miles walked swiftly, the pain in his side throbbing but not unbearable. He was just a mile from the parking lot and he slowed his pace, touching his ribs. He'd be fine.

As he headed down the trail, Abert's squirrels jumped from tree to tree, their tufted ears flopping. Several ravens announced his presence to one another, and a couple of nuthatches pecked at the pine bark, searching for a lunch of bugs.

His mind wandered again to the woman and that black dog with the underbite. He wondered what Madeline's story was. And if she was going to stay in Flagstaff, could they be friends? At least friends?

"Whoa, whoa, man," he said aloud. "You just met her, for God's sake!"

Still, he wondered if she would be going back to Caboose Coffee any time soon. And, if so, might she be there at the same time he was? A guy on a day off sure deserved a mocha, right?

"If I see her, I see her. If I don't, I don't."

Wow. He was channeling Hemingway with those short, memorable sentences! He'd better just zoom home and capture it all in his journal. But not before he got that cup of coffee. Then, he'd get himself out into the woods for a night of camping before reporting to work the next morning.

He'd take a shower when he got home and then, well, the coffee shop was calling his name. And maybe not just his.

Chapter 9

Harold Boyle trudged up the long hill toward the Flagstaff observatory. It was a nice day, and he stopped at the lookout that shared a long view of the town and university. The city was small but spread out, with the white university sports dome bright in the autumn sunlight. Two trains dissected the town, one traveling west, the other east. Harold remembered the constant sound of trains passing through town and the conductors blowing the train whistle way too often. But now the trains seemed quieter, or, rather, the whistles were apparently gone. Could that be right? He turned to finish walking up to the observatory.

Someone named Charlie had found his handyman card on the bulletin board at Lacy's coffee shop, which from what Harold could tell was a mix of workmen like him and snot-nosed college kids and their professors. Not that he cared. The fact that he'd put his newly printed card out and it had got him a possible job was not bad. Not bad at all. He'd put one there and one at another coffee place, Caboose Coffee, and sure enough they were doing the trick. A cup of fancy coffee may cost five bucks these days, but the shops were turning out to be good for business—his business.

He pushed open the heavy observatory doors and was delivered to Charlie by a stooped older man. Charlie ended up being a woman. "You okay on ladders?" she asked him, barely making eye contact. Harold knew the look. She was either on pain medication or high on something else. Probably the legal stuff, since she had such a big job.

"Yeah, I am. What's the job?"

She told him the regular cleaners didn't do windows, the company that usually did them was overbooked, and that she needed them done in the next three days because of school tours coming through.

They agreed on a price, she told him where the longest ladders were, and he left, with an agreement to get started the next day. Easy job, and not bad money. He was back on top.

Chapter 10

Maddy finished her introductory email to the local food group and hit, "Send."

She reviewed her hostess application for the Italian restaurant Mama Patrice's and hit "Send" again.

That was it. She'd applied to a dozen jobs, most part-time. Good for now.

After all, with the Mercedes windfall, along with the money she'd kept in her own accounts to which Arthur had neither knowledge nor access—thank God she'd listened to Belinda—she was good for a few months before having to find a job.

And even if most of the jobs she applied to were not ones where she could be traced on the Internet, she could tell already she would not be all right with staying shut in or closed off from people. She wanted her life back—her pre-Arthur life.

Somehow, she had allowed herself to let go of her friends from before Arthur. She had not even realized then that she had done that. She had fallen for him hard and made a life with him based on his expectations and life. But that had not worked either.

Only six months into their marriage, which initially was both sweet and exciting, at nearly every social event (his), she had done something wrong, done something that bothered him. At first, he was just "concerned" with her behavior ("Darling, you must see that you were paying that waiter too much attention.”). Eventually, though, everything she did made him angry and, over time, his anger turned violent.

“I do not appreciate the way you were leaning into my young associate, so obviously flirting in front of my entire staff,” he told her after one of his end-of-year office parties.

“I have no idea what you’re talking about,” she said.

The first slap took her by total surprise. The first of many over the next several months.

Then, even when she befriended one of his female lawyers, it sent him over the edge.

“She is a slut, and you are becoming just like her.” Smack!

She was so astounded the first time he hit her she believed it was just the mistaken impulse of someone with a big job under pressure. A judge, he *did* have a big job in the community.

But it was not a one-time occurrence, as he’d promised her with roses and dinner out at a tiny place overlooking Lake Michigan after the first smack.

“I saw you smiling at that guy at the bar like you wanted to fuck him right then and there,” he said out of the blue after they had stopped for a bite to eat one Saturday night.

She was shocked, as usual, when they got home and he not only hit her but threw her down on their bed and took her. It was weeks before she could even admit it to herself: Raped her.

The next night, all apologies, he handed her the keys to a brand-new Mercedes, and she recognized it for what it was: a bribe. But though Arthur’s gesture was not little, it was too late. Way too late.

Because it happened again, and then again, and she knew she had to get away from Arthur Dempster. Get back—or, rather, move forward—into her own life, a life separate from him. Forever separate.

The sounds of sirens screaming west on Route 66 brought her back to the present. She wondered what the emergency was.

She stopped herself from thinking yet again of how she could have let it happen, how he had wooed her into his life, his world, his abuse. Yes, she had to admit to herself she had been in an abusive marriage.

Now she went back to Craigslist Flagstaff, and clicked on Housing Available—dog friendly only, of course. Finding housing was the next step to becoming a permanent resident of this sweet mountain town. She was safe now, away from Arthur by nearly two thousand miles, and by growing emotional distance, too.

She read about a couple possible apartments for rent, and then clicked on an ad for a small house in someone's backyard. Now that looked just about perfect. She would check it out tomorrow, crossing her fingers that this would be the next piece falling into place on her sometimes puzzling journey.

Flagstaff would help her get her back on her feet, back to herself.

Chapter 11

Miles rode toward downtown, relaxed after his two-day break. Something caught his eye as he coasted down Beaver Street. He braked. On the side of a small shop was graffiti—unusual for this neighborhood. "STOP THE INVASION" alongside a crudely drawn noose.

What the hell? He'd call Luis Ortega after he got to work.

He walked back into the paper, amazed how good it had felt to completely disconnect from work and from the world of news. Except for his aching ribs, and the creepiness of the graffiti, he felt refreshed and ready to hit it.

He pushed through the half-door that swung open, and Butch walked quickly over to him before Miles had a chance to turn into the newsroom.

"Dude, Ruthless is on the war path. She's absolutely steaming at you."

"Wait. What? I haven't even been here."

"Exactly. There was a murder up on Mars Hill—somewhere around the observatory. She needed you to cover it, but you were MIA. I even stopped by your place to try and find you, but no go. I hope wherever you went to or whoever you were with was worth it, big time." Butch turned back to his desk as both men heard the angry voice of Ruth calling Miles's name. "Just a head's up."

"Right. Thanks, man," Miles said. He turned toward the wrath of his editor, the pain in his ribs and the graffiti forgotten.

Walking into the newsroom, he patted his pockets in search of that elusive cell phone. He wondered again if it had slid off the mountainside or if it was somewhere at his place. Stuck between the couch pillows? He'd used his landline to talk with his mom the day he got off work. Unlike many of his generation, Miles was not obsessively attached to his cell phone. In fact, he hated being always accessible to anyone in his life—but now realized what a mistake he'd made by not being better about staying connected with his boss and his newsroom. He went to Ruth's work area.

"I heard you were trying to reach me. What's this about a killing?"

Ruth's face flushed, and her eyes flashed. He was so caught up in trying to figure out how he'd lost his cell phone that he didn't hear her first response.

"Sorry, what?"

"I said, *sit down*, Miles." She nodded to the neon green hard plastic chair beside her desk.

Miles sat, but not before noticing the smirk he was getting from Nathan Cawdry, the sports editor.

"If I weren't so short staffed, you'd be fuckin' history," Ruth exploded. "The biggest story of the year, and you're incognito. Reporters can take a couple days off, but they can *not* go off-grid without telling their editors how to reach them. Which you told me I would be able to do."

"And I meant it. I really did." That sounded weak even to him.

"That's why the paper issued you a damn cell phone in the first place."

"I know, I know. But, to tell you the truth, I think I lost it over the side of Mt. Elden. I went hiking up there and I slid down—"

"Save the self-serving dramatics, Miles." She rummaged in her desk drawer.

"I'm really, really sorry. I had no idea something so big was going on. Should I go—"

He stopped when he saw what Ruth was holding. A generic cell phone that looked a whole lot like his. In fact, there was the telltale scratch on the side of the phone. Did someone miraculously turn it in after finding it up on Mt. Elden? He thought very briefly about exaggerating his slide off the mountain top but decided that wasn't the right approach.

"Are you missing something?" she asked, her eyes boring holes into his.

"Um, okay. I'll bite. Where was it?"

"The first time I called you, I heard a faint, very faint sound of some tinny electric guitars and some old bastards singing, 'I'd feel a bunch better.' I thought maybe the sports guys had turned on an oldies radio station and didn't pay much attention to it—didn't connect it to my dialing your number. Can you guess what happened after that?"

Miles could. He glanced at his disastrous desk.

"It's not 'I'd feel a bunch better.' "

"What?" Ruth's voice was a growl.

"The song is 'I'll Feel A Whole Lot Better.' "

He knew he should shut up now, but he didn't.

"The Byrds, '65."

"Damn it, Miles," Ruth exploded. "I don't give a

rat's ass if it's the Byrds or the Stones or Taylor fuckin' Swift. The damn song could be your swan song, if it was up to me. And the ring tone you selected was chosen for the cell phone that actually belongs to the *Gazette,* don't forget. The point is, it's got to be on your person for it to be any use to us."

"Sorry, sorry. Then what happened?"

Always a sucker for a good story, and his boss seemed intent on telling it her way.

"I left you a message saying we needed you to come in pronto, that there's been a murder up at the observatory A woman's apparently been dead a couple of days, but they only discovered her body yesterday. When I didn't hear back from you or see your scrawny-bearded face, I called again. And again. Finally I realized every time I dialed you, there was the same sad song."

Miles bit his tongue. Not a good time to argue musical tastes. Definitely not.

"So Cawdry hears me leaving you messages and puts two and two together. He motions me over to that side of the newsroom, and nods toward your desk. Your filthy desk."

" 'Dial again, Ruth, would you?' he asks me. "So I do, and then there's the 1960's sound track again, coming from under your pile of garbage. Cawdry, the new copy editor, and I start sifting through the papers and notebooks and what all, and there's your phone singing away all over again."

Singing like a Byrd, Miles thought but bit his tongue.

"Now you listen and you listen good, Miles. I stormed into the publisher's office with the intent to fire you, but for whatever reason, he said to give you one more chance. And, given that we're short so many people and are under a hiring freeze, I had to agree. But you are on probation, got it? Through the end of the damn year, and then we'll reassess. But you are skating on *extremely* thin ice here."

"Yes, okay, thanks. I understand. And, again, for what it's worth, I'm really, really sorry."

"That does not cut it. Just do your job and we'll see if we want to keep you, come the end of your probation."

"So tell me what to do. Shall I go up Mars Hill and talk to Charlie now?"

"When Kalisha, the new reporter-slash-copy-editor, comes back from her second morning on cops, you will sit down with her, find out everything she knows, and the two of you will write a story. Then you can go up to the observatory and take Kalisha with you. You read the police log yesterday with the report on the killing, didn't you?"

His red face was her answer.

"Good *God,* Miles. I thought you were a true newspaper man with blue ink running through your veins. That's one of the reasons you work here. But I guess that explains why you didn't call in. If you *had* read it and ignored it, I suppose I'd be even angrier than I am now. I hope you got a good vacation in Fiji or some other exotic place."

"I don't know where the two days went to, boss, er, Ruth. I was mostly out on the trails, and then went camping last night in the Coconino National Forest. Not that this is an excuse but even if I'd had my phone with me, it would probably been out of range, and—"

"Save it, Miles."

"Sorry, sorry. I really am. It won't happen again. You have my word."

"If it does, don't bother coming into work the next day. Murder or no murder, we'll handle it without you," she said, turning to her computer indicating the conversation was over. Or almost over.

"And by the end of the day, after you've done your work, I want that desk *completely* cleaned up. Journalists need to be organized. And so I want to see the cell phone clipped to your belt on a cell-phone holder. You do wear a damn belt, don't you, Harper?"

"From now on, Ruth," he answered, happy to note that she was now calling him by his last name again, a sign that she might be thawing. "Promise."

"You screwed up bad, Harper," she said.

Badly, he thought but thank God did not say. His tongue would be positively bloody soon.

"And follow up on this as well," she said, handing him a note on a narrow piece of lined paper. "Check it out with Butch in Advertising."

Miles took the paper and turned away.

"Forgetting something?" Ruth asked.

He turned back to see her holding up his phone. He took it, feeling his face reddening again, walked over to Advertising, and then outside with Butch.

"Thanks again for the head's up," Miles said as they stood on the sidewalk in front of the newspaper, Butch lighting up a Marlboro light.

Light or not, it was still a cancer stick, Miles thought.

"You toast, Dude?"

"I'm on probation for the rest of the year."

"Good of her, the queen bitch of the newsroom," Butch said, glancing behind him as if afraid she could hear through mortar and brick. "Don't know how you stand her. All the other department heads completely loathe the sight of Ruthless. Even the sound of her voice makes them crazy."

"I like working for her," Miles said, suddenly realizing how true that was. He wondered not for the first time if the fact that Ruth was a woman over forty and a boss was why many of the *Gazette*'s male employees resented her. She was the only woman in a management position, in a classic good-old-boy system. Miles had always found her to be fair and direct, and he wanted to make it right. He needed to make it right. "She's just got an edge, is all. So what's with this note you gave her?"

Butch blew a couple of smoke rings into the air and said some guy had come in asking for a reporter to talk to about the observatory up on Mars Hill.

"He claimed he could give some background about the place, and blah blah blah. Seemed like one of those hangers-on who sniffs around certain stories. Did not seem at all legit."

"Got a description?"

"Regular looking, I guess. Not tall, not short."

Miles groaned internally.

"Got a phone number?" he asked not too hopefully as they walked back into the building.

"Sorry, Dude, but it was crazy busy," Butch said, and looked over at his desk, where his phone was ringing. "Better take this call."

Miles knew most walk-ins had less information than they claimed. But in his mind, it was always worth a follow-up call. He remembered one of his favorite features stories was about an elderly woman who grew a giant pumpkin—eighty pounds. She and her husband had met in kindergarten, lived a couple of blocks from the newspaper, and he'd walked in to brag about his wife of sixty years. Miles was the only reporter who wanted to check it out. The pumpkin eventually won first place at the county fair, ended up as a page-one story, and won Miles first place in feature stories from the Associated Press Club that year. So there! He learned later that the couple—who had him over for pie and ice cream—had his framed story hanging over their living room couch. Now *that* walk-in was worth it. Miles went back to his work area and saw Nick Cawdry on the phone rolling his eyes at him, nodding toward Miles's desk.

Yup. It was a mess. A serious mess he'd have to get control of if he wanted to keep his job. His *fuckin'* job. And he did. He really, really did.

He was about to start on that when a woman he'd not seen before walked into the newsroom. Kalisha, the new *Gazette* colleague. She was probably five foot six, oval face, dark brown skin and hair, and muscles that Miles could see even through her outdoor jacket. He knew Ruth had pushed the publisher to get her hired during the freeze and had only convinced him after three people left the *Gazette* for greener—or at least different—pastures. Plus, like most news outlets, the *Gazette* was much whiter than its readers. Diversity was much needed.

Happily, Miles left behind the job of his messy workstation, walked over to Kalisha, extending his hand in greeting. She had a strong handshake, and he had to hide his surprise or, rather, his grimace.

She smiled at him, and, looking over at his disaster of a desk, nodded toward hers.

"We'd better work over here where we can find a computer," she quipped.

"I'm Miles," he said following her over to her workstation.

"I deduced that, being a reporter and all," she joked. "I'm Kalisha, I go by Lisha, and we've got one hell of a story here. Why don't you type, and I'll read to you from my notes?"

Miles could tell immediately that he was going to like working with this woman whose handshake would put most WWE wrestlers to shame. They sat down in front of her computer and got to work.

Chapter 12

"Here's the scoop," Kalisha said.

Miles's fingers flew over the keyboard, as he wondered if she was being ironic or really talked like some old-school journalist.

"They haven't ID'd the woman yet," he typed as Kalisha looked at her reporter's notebook. "Her body was found in the Mars Hill woods, but it looks like she may have been killed inside the Percival Telescope room—is it called a refractor? Apparently, it's been closed to the public for viewing the past month for repairs."

"Blood? Signs of struggle?"

"Yes on blood, no on an obvious struggle. The official line is they're not saying what she was doing there, given that it was closed. But a kid working in the gift shop told me—off the record—he heard it was a cleaning woman."

She glanced down at her notes, trying to decipher her handwriting, and saw Miles watching her.

"I've got audio, too, of course, but just want to give you the quickest version," she explained.

"Right. I'm the same way—use both handwritten notes and a recording," he said.

A decade ago, it had only been the TV and radio reporters who used recording equipment. Now at news conferences, all you saw were digital records and a dying number of pens and paper.

"The kid told me if I said anything about it, he'd probably get canned."

"How'd you get him to talk to you in the first place?"

"I saw him watching from outside the group of observatory bigwigs and the other media," she said. "You know how it is sometimes. You just get this sense that somebody has something they want to say, even if they don't know it themselves. Right before he went back into the observatory's main building, he looked upset. After a bit, I followed him inside."

"Good for you. Any of the other media talk to him?"

"No. Or, at least not while I was there. But I kind of doubt it. Everybody was focused on talking to the brass. And so even though I knew I was running late getting back to the paper, I followed him to the visitors' center gift shop, and that's when he spilled. Not that he knew anything big about it, but still. After we file this story, I think we should go back up there and confirm the identity with—" She paused and checked her notes. "—Charlotte, is it? The slack, er, I mean flack."

"She goes by Charlie," Miles said, appreciating his colleague's joke. He thought about the woman he'd nearly slept with when he first arrived at the *Gazette.* Before she crossed over to the dark side of public relations—a flack.

"You with me, Miles?"

"Yeah, sorry. Nice work on the kid. He say anything else?"

"That's just it. He whispered to me that he'd heard rumors that something illegal was going on at the observatory."

"Wait, what? I can hardly hear those two phrases together in once sentence: Illegal and the Flagstaff observatory," Miles said.

"He had just said the word *illegal,* when a bunch of observatory bigwigs walked back inside and past the gift shop. At that point, he clammed up, except to show me some of the items for sale, as if I were a rich tourist."

"I'm in love with that place," Miles said. "Riding up Mars Hill during the day, but also at night for the star and planet viewing."

"Believe me, I know all about the planets—or at least I will," Lisha said.

"Huh?"

"I ended up spending a fortune at the Visitors' Center once some of the people started coming in after the press conference ended. You know, to cover for the kid. I don't think Charlotte or anyone else noticed it was me in there. After deadline, I'll show you what I bought."

"Anything else?" Miles asked.

"Let me see. The cops were called when the security guy opened up the telescope building in the morning—it's temporarily closed to the public right now, which is why they didn't find her until a day or two after she was killed. Anyway, he saw what he thought was blood near the viewing platform, almost as if she was, here's a direct quote 'looking up at the heavens' when she was murdered, he told police. Amazing quote, eh? But her body wasn't found there but about three hundred yards away in a copse of"—she frowned at her notes—"gamble oak trees. Is that correct?"

"Right. G-A-M-B-E-L. How was she killed?"

"Five stab wounds into her chest and neck. A detective Ortega—Louis?—said it showed anger, but then I got the feeling he stopped himself before saying too much."

She flipped the page. "The only other thing I noticed was that the woman Charlotte Thompson—Charlie, is it? Seemed a hell of a lot more upset than most flacks ever show. In my experience, anyway."

"I know Charlie. She used to be a TV reporter. She moved over to the dark side a couple of years ago," Miles joked.

Lisha smiled, understanding his reference to public relations versus journalism. Newspaper reporters often felt judgmental when it came to TV reporters but were positively holier-than-thou about any kind of journalists who switched to public relations.

"She was good. I mean really, really good. I was shocked when she took the job at the observatory—though I love the place as I already told ya. It just took me by surprise. She used to continually scoop me on stories for the local television station. So I guess I should be lucky we're no longer competing. In fact, the TV station is no more."

Miles's phone rang.

"And it's *Luis* Ortega," he said, and then answered his phone.

"Miles, it's me, Charlie."

"Hey, Charlie," he said as he raised his eyebrows at Lisha. "What's up?"

"I need to talk with you about the murder story."

"Okay. I can be up there in a little bit. Say an

hour?"

Miles hung up.

Ruth's voice bellowed through the newsroom.

"I asked you two to work on the story together, not do a fuckin' mind meld," she shouted. "Send me that copy."

"Will do," Miles answered, turning back to his new colleague.

"You want to write this up, and I'll cover the observatory background, and get Flagstaff's murder rates—stuff you can add to the piece?"

"Let's do it."

After they wrote the story, mixing the details of the murder and observatory details, they sent it over to Ruth, who edited it for Page 1 layout.

"Show and tell time," Lisha announced. While she and Miles waited for Ruth's feedback, she proudly opened an observatory gift bag to reveal a mobile of planets.

"With this thing hanging somewhere in my apartment, I'll be a planet scientist in no time," she quipped. "I love that Pluto is part of this."

"For sure," Miles said. Like many people in Flagstaff, they were both aware that the townspeople resented the fact that Pluto had been demoted from planet to dwarf planet in 2006. It had been discovered by Clyde Tombaugh at the Flagstaff observatory in 1930, and for all those years had been considered the ninth planet in the solar system. Rightfully so, if you talked to locals.

Miles walked over to Ruth and told her about the call from Charlie.

"Okay, you'd better get up there. And good job,

you two," she said as Kalisha joined them. "Kalisha, I wanted to show you a few things on the editing end, but you should go with Miles to the observatory for a possible follow-up first. Meet me back here by, let's say, three, and I'll take you through the ropes."

"You can call me Lisha."

"Okay, Lisha," Ruth said.

Outside, Miles hopped on his bike.

"Meet you up there, Lisha," he said, and rode toward Mars Hill. Kalisha drove by in a dark green Volvo wagon and tapped the horn as she passed him.

Chapter 13

No media trucks were parked outside the observatory, Miles was relieved to see. As he'd told Kalisha, since Charlie left news reporting, he and the *Gazette* didn't have much competition. But you never knew when new journalists might end up in town, young and eager. While he used to long for the city life, now he felt lucky to be here instead of the high-paced life of the city and too often cut-throat journalism. After locking up his bike, he passed the empty Volvo and walked up the steps of the observatory.

Inside the building, he immediately felt the sweat from his ride chill against his back. He pulled his sticky shirt away from his skin, combed his hair with his fingers, and stopped in front of the information desk.

An older man Miles hadn't met gave him a toothy smile.

"Help you, son?"

The man was tall, even sitting you could tell, with a horsey face, and long teeth to match. His black hair going to gray was slicked back in the fashion of his youth, and half-glasses were smeared with fingerprints and dust. A paperclip was holding one side of the frames together.

"I'm with the *Daily Gazette,* and I wanted to talk to—"

"You're here for Charlotte, I know. Your colleague

Lisa is in there with her," said the man whose nametag read "Beez."

"It's Lisha," Miles said, but Beez was reaching for the phone and did not respond.

"I'll just buzz Charlotte to say you're joining them."

"Thanks. I'm Miles Harper. Thanks, uh, Beez, is it?"

"That's me," Beez said, tapping his nametag as if to congratulate Miles on his reading skills. "Irwin Beasely, but most everybody calls me Beez. Since I was a kid, you know."

He picked up the phone, but Miles interrupted.

"So, Mr. Beasley—"

"Beez."

"So, Beez, can I ask you a question before you call Charlie—Charlotte?"

"You *may* ask me a question, Miles. And you probably *can*, too."

Miles smiled. That was the kind of language correction he did all the time.

"If I *may* ask you, did you know the woman who died?"

"Was kilt, more like it," Beez said, resting his hand on the phone receiver, which was back in its cradle. "Just met her one night when I came in late cuz I went and left my readin' glasses behind at work."

He looked at Miles to see if that needed any explanation. Seeing that it didn't, he continued, his words gushing like an untamed river.

"We just said hello, like, is all. I asked her how her night was going and introduced myself—she had a hard time with the word Beez now, didn't she—and we talked like you do with someone you don't share a language with. I said *Buenos noches,* and she said *Good bye,* you know, both tryin'. And, sure. Didn't I like that about her? She seemed a sweet girl and was scrubbin' the floors in the hallway real careful, like."

He took a breath but kept going before Miles could say a word.

"And then yesterday don't the police find her body not far from the viewing station, in a bunch of trees. Said she'd been murdered with a knife. Not that they told me any of that, but I heard some talk on the police radio when one of them walked through the lobby on the way to talk to Director Stenalp."

He paused for another big breath, and Miles saw tears in his eyes. But inside Miles's head, a voice whispered, *Are they real?*

"Now I ask ya. Who in this dang world would want to kill a cleanin' lady who was just doin' her job? Just new to town, I hear."

He stared at Miles, as if the younger man might have the answers.

"Don't know, Beez. But I hope the police will suss out the killer."

"Yessirree, I do, too. I sure do, too."

Miles noticed scratches on the man's hands and on his face.

"You been attacked by a kitten?" he asked, nodding at the scratches.

"I raise roses," he said, after a beat. "This time of year, I cut them way back, of course. But like an idiot I went out there without my gardening gloves or hat. Was distracted. You know, after hearin' about that young woman."

Beez picked up the phone again, conversation over, indicated the hallway behind him with his chin, and Miles heard him tell Charlie he was on the way.

Miles found Charlie in her tidy office, talking with Lisha, who sat across the desk from her.

"*There* you are, Miles Harper," Charlie said, stood up to her five-foot height, and waved her hand toward an empty chair beside Lisha. Miles knew she often wore shoe lifts to look taller. As opposed to his boss Ruth, who seemed to relish both her diminutive stature and her high-heel collection—perhaps making up for it with all her cursing.

Miles leaned in to shake her hand and sat down. He noticed a tightness around Charlie's eyes that seemed new. She had fly-away auburn hair, a smile that today appeared forced, and brown eyes that looked stressed.

"I was just about to fill Lisa in on the latest," Charlie said.

"It's Lisha, short for Kalisha," Lisha said flatly, obviously familiar with correcting this.

"Oh, sorry," Charlie apologized without looking at Kalisha.

Miles saw Lisha's digital recorder was on, so he simply took out his notebook, flipping it open to the first blank page.

"I'm not sure why I'm telling you this because I could keep it to myself," she began, and both Miles and Lisha looked up expectantly. "But I want to be transparent, even though it would normally be the police who would release this information."

She paused, gazing at Miles as if for some words—of appreciation?

"Okay," he said.

"Okay. During the search, police found a few packets of what looks like cocaine in the cleaning-supply closet. As I told the police, Feliciana Garcia and her husband Juan had been working here for nearly a decade. A family cleaning business. But her sister Alejandra Lopez had just been helping out only recently. Just since last week. And then, as you know, her dead body was discovered on the grounds."

Body, not dead body, Miles thought but didn't say. That was one of the random Associated Press rules he remembered from his university journalism classes. Saying *a body* implies the person is dead. A *dead* body is redundant. He pulled himself out of his head and turned his attention back to Charlie.

"So while I can say with one hundred percent certainty that Feliciana is not a drug user and she swears her sister was not one either, I did not know her—Alejandra."

Miles wondered why Charlie was telling them all this. As she had said, normally the press would get something like this from the cop shop. Why was it in her interest to tell them? He was glad Lisha was there so he could ask her later what she thought.

Suddenly, an image of the woman Madeline jumped into his mind, and he imagined them talking it over, at his house. *What the hell, get a grip, man!*

He saw that both women were looking at him now.

"I'm sorry, what?" he said.

"I said I wanted to ask a few questions," Lisha said.

"Oh, right," Miles said, studying his reporter's notebook to cover his embarrassment. "Go for it, Lisha."

"Where was Alejandra visiting from?" Lisha asked, looking at Charlie.

"Mexico. She's a Mexican citizen."

"And her sister and family?"

"They've got dual citizenship, and have all their papers in order," Charlie said.

"Is she, was she, a visitor or an undocumented worker?" Miles joined the conversation.

"I do not *know*, Miles," Charlie answered, exasperated. "The police are looking into all of this. I just wanted to give you a head's up on the cocaine we found."

"How much was there?" Lisha asked.

"I do not really know," Charlie said, her gaze turning to the window.

"Well, was it a sale-able amount or private usage amount?" Miles pushed.

"I do not *know.*"

"Okay. And from what Lisha reported on in today's story, she was killed working the graveyard shift?"

He heard the awful choice of phrase as soon as the words were out of his mouth.

Both women groaned.

"Sorry," he said quickly. "Didn't mean that the way it came out."

"She was killed between one and three a.m., the M.E. thought," said Lisha, looking at her notes. She was referring to the Medical Examiner, the person responsible for identifying cause of death, and reporting to the police any deaths that did not appear natural. "The police say the family didn't call in a missing-person's report for two days." Lisha looked at her notes again. “Maybe because she was here illegally?”

They were all quiet for several seconds.

“Ever met her?” Miles asked.

“Miles, I already told you I had not,” Charlie answered, voice testy. “I had no idea we even had a new person cleaning, not that I ever would, really. I’ve only met Feliciana a couple, three, times when I was working overtime on some big projects.”

“So why are you telling us about the coke, Charlie? I mean, I don’t understand why you would.”

“Listen, Miles—and Kalisha—the reason I called you is, well, the police will tell you all about the cocaine being discovered, if in fact that’s how it’s identified,” she said, her words feeling rushed as she stared out the window at the ponderosa pines. “And we do not want that to get out right now.”

She turned back to Miles, and he thought he saw a pleading in her tired eyes. “I’m not saying it won’t come out, of course not. We know it will. But as you know we’re having this huge fundraiser for the Discovery telescope that ends with a big celebration next week. There are giant donors—I mean humungous potential donors—coming to the event. Some are on the fence about their donations—they always are. And if this information got out now, well, that could just put them on the wrong side of that fence.”

She sat back in her chair and sighed. Miles thought Charlie seemed exhausted but was probably relieved to have spit out her request.

He sighed, too. Because he hated this with a passion.

“Look, Charlie, we can’t keep this kind of information out of the paper. You of all people know that. Our responsibility is to the reader, the audience, but not to the people or in this case the institutions we report on," he said.

He was disappointed, no, shocked, that Charlie would ask this of them. She knew better.

"I do not need a damn Journalism 101 lecture, Miles," she snapped. "But what if the cocaine was a random thing, unrelated to the murder?"

"You're saying what, exactly?"

Charlie hesitated, then spoke.

"I need to say something to you, Miles, off the record."

Miles and Lisha exchanged a look, but Lisha did not make a move to leave.

"Okay, we can go off the record for a minute," he said.

Both reporters put down their pens, and Lisha pushed "pause" on the recorder.

"It's like this, Miles. I think we have an employee who's a bit over his head in cocaine," she said, again choosing her words carefully. "I think the finding of the powder was a total coincidence. Honestly. A fluke. The director is putting this person on probation if he agrees to get counseling. So I think that's completely unrelated to the visiting cleaning woman who went and got herself killed."

Miles was surprised at her unsympathetic phrase.

Leaning forward over her desktop, as if fighting against strong winds, Charlie appealed directly to Miles.

"If there's any connection, any at all, the police will obviously find it and it will be public information—and rightfully so, of course. But until then—and please both of you just forget what I said about the fundraiser, that was a ridiculous detail I should not have shared—I do not see how it serves your readers to connect the two, even subtly."

"But it was found with the cleaning stuff you said," Lisha noted. "That isn't significant?"

Charlie leaned back in her chair, the winds suddenly calm.

"Not a clue," Charlie responded, sounding deflated.

The three sat in silence for a full minute, and then Miles spoke.

"I'll have to share this with Ruth," he said.

"Of course," Charlie said. "But I just ask that you state my case—and forget about the fundraiser. Again, I know how stupid that was. And I apologize to both of you for that."

"Can't promise anything," Miles told her.

"I know, I know," she snapped.

Charlie stood up and waited not so patiently for them to gather their things. The two reporters walked out into the sunshine.

"She's the PR person you said was a former reporter, and a really good one?" Lisha asked, her voice incredulous. They stood in the parking lot. "Is she for real?"

Miles nodded, wondering what the hell was going on with Charlie, with the observatory.

"I think you even called her a straight shooter. I can't believe she asked us to sign on with this garbage," Lisha said, incensed. "Cover up for her fundraising, for Lord's sake."

Miles was dumbfounded, too. He climbed onto his bike and clipped on his helmet.

"I'll meet you below," he said. "We might end up holding it, though."

"You are *not* serious," she said. "Lying is something my mama *never* let us get away with. You could see she was bald-faced lying."

"We'll talk to Ruth."

Charlie watched the two reporters from her window. She did not want to lie to Miles, but she certainly could not tell the truth. She thought of her dealer Frank-man, and a chill ran through her entire body. She felt a lump in her throat and turned away from the window. A toot would help.

Miles glided down the hill, thinking.

He was pretty sure how this would go down with Ruthless. Pretty damn sure.

Chapter 14

After running on the trail behind the MoMo, Maddy left Daisy in the room and walked down to the lobby where Karan and Tan sat behind the counter. From outside, it appeared they were deep in discussion, but they stopped talking when she opened the door. Tan nodded curtly at her and stomped out, nearly slamming the door behind him.

Karan's eyes held a touch of sadness. Maddy had talked with Karan more than a few times before or after her walks or runs with Daisy, and she had enjoyed his company, even in such a fleeting way. She was sure he looked a little off today.

"Miss Maddy, how good to see you," he said, an unlit cigarette between his second and middle fingers. "Tell me. How is your room treating you?"

"It's been great, Karan." She hesitated. "Everything okay with Tan? Not that it's my business."

"Oh, he's fine, thank you."

"He seemed a little stressed."

"You are a perceptive woman, Miss Maddy," Karan said slowly. "But I do not want to bother you with my little problems."

"No bother, Karan. Really."

"Well," he said, hesitating. "I will just say I am worried about Tanak. But I believe that most parents of teenagers feel the same way, my wife has told me."

"I have heard that, too."

"Do you know that Tanak means the 'Prize' in Hindi?"

"How beautiful. You know when I met both your kids when I first arrived here, they were so sweet to me, and so helpful."

"Yes, they are good children. But lately Tanak hardly talks to me, and not even much to his mother, with whom he has always been so close," he said, shaking his head. "We no longer know who his friends are. They used to all come to the house, but no longer. And his grades have fallen. He received the first B of his life."

Karan turned the cigarette over and over in his fingers.

"All A's and one B? That sounds pretty good to me," Maddy said.

"Not in my family. His teachers tell my wife he has not been focused in class this past month. And same for my daughter—and she is less talkative than she always has been."

Karan glanced back at the door where his son had left.

"My wife went through his things, afraid she might find drugs. Nothing, though."

He seemed to catch himself and stopped talking for a moment.

"Sorry for your worries," Maddy said.

"Oh, just probably the silly concerns of a father," he said. "Also, I am quitting smoking, and this makes everything worse. I admit it is a challenge for me."

"Good luck with that."

"So now that you have listened to me go on and on,

what is it I can do for you?"

"I wanted to let you know I found a place to live—a little house not far from downtown. A neighborhood they call Hospital Hill?"

"Oh, that is a nice area," he said. "And while we will be sorry to lose you, I am happy you will no longer be living in a motel. When do you move out?"

"Next weekend, if that is okay."

"Of course, of course. And please accept one free night with us," he said, holding up his hand when Maddy opened her mouth to protest. "My family likes to do that for some of our best guests. So your bill will be reduced by one night."

"Oh, Karan, that is so nice of you all."

"The only thing we ask in return is that you write a review on Google or TripAdvising.com, one of those."

Maddy hesitated.

"Let me think about that, Karan."

His eyebrows rose in surprise, but he collected himself.

"Of course, of course. It is not required of you, Miss Maddy."

"It's just that, well, I do not want to tell the world my whereabouts," she added, feeling like a jerk.

"I understand," Karan said, and Maddy thought he was remembering her request of privacy when she arrived last month.

When she left the lobby, she scolded herself. She could write an anonymous review, and Arthur would be no more the wiser. Right? Of course.

She grabbed Daisy and walked toward Caboose Coffee, noticing again the trains headed east and west like some giant birds' migration pattern.

Chapter 15

Halfway down Mars Hill, the flip phone rang in his pocket.

"Yeah."

"Oh, hello, is this Mr. Boyle, the handyman?" asked a whispery voice.

"That's me." he answered.

"Oh, hello, Mr. Boyle. I am Mrs. Gerald Naderman, and a young friend who saw your name in a coffee shop downtown passed it on to me."

"Yeah, that's me," he repeated.

"Well, sir, I have some weeds that need pulling in my yard, and a cleaning project, and I wonder if you are available?"

"I've got another job right now. But I should be done with that in just a couple of days. Can I come by at the end of the week? You can show me what you want done."

"That would be splendid. If you could bring along a letter of reference from your past employers, I'd appreciate that, too."

"Okay," he said. Maybe that Charlie woman would vouch for him after he finished with those windows. He'd better make them shine big time.

"Splendid. Then I will see you Thursday or Friday, Mr. Boyle. Please call me before you come, so I can be certain to be here upon your arrival."

"I'll do that."

Harold hung up and smiled. Maybe Flagstaff would be a good fit for him after all. Sure seemed like his luck was changing.

Harold, you never know how things will end up, his dead mother whispered in his head.

"Right, Ma," he answered. "How right you are."

The day after finishing the observatory job, Harold turned into the narrow path to Mrs. Naderman's. The house was small, but well built, he could see. Unlike his mother's old place in California, through which the wind came whistling through the cracks, he guessed this one would handle any kind of a violent storm. He saw lace curtains twitch in the front room. Then there she was, a pink-faced woman with dark lipstick and a white-haired perm at the front door. Upper crust, his mother would have called her.

"Mr. Boyle?" She held out her wrinkled hand and he shook it lightly.

"Yeah, that's me."

"Good of you to come. Let me show you the weeds out back," she said, pulling the door closed behind her and walking in front of him to the back yard. Tiny white flowers on some kind of ground vine were taking over her lawn. "Are you experienced in gardening or landscaping?"

"Not much. But I sure can drive a lawn mower and pull up those weeds."

"That would be grand. I have a hand mower, and I am proud to tell you that it still works well after three decades."

"Okay. And you said you had some other work?"

"My windows want cleaning—from the outside.

Can you do that for me as well?"

"I just finished a job up at the observatory cleaning their windows."

"Oh, wonderful," she said, walking him back to the front of the house. "And do you have that letter I requested?"

"The woman up there, goes by Charlie, said she'd have one for me but she hasn't been around much this week. I'll call her tomorrow. That okay?"

"All right," Ethel said. "Meanwhile, could you get the mowing and weeding done today, and then move on to the windows? It would be grand if you had those done in a week's time. I have a new tenant, and I would like the place to look a bit more sharp with her here."

She told him where to find the lawn mower and ladder and went back inside.

Boyle got to work.

Chapter 16

"She asked you to fuckin' what?"

Ruth was standing near the Mr. Coffee, filling the orange plastic UNA to-go cup with her fourth cup of the day, adding three teaspoons of sugar and a dollop of half and half. In her polished high heels, she was still nearly a head shorter than Miles, though her spikey hair—with this week's blue tips—gave her a couple extra inches. She, Lisha, and Miles were in the cramped break room adjacent to the huge printing press. It smelled of boiled coffee and ink.

"To hold off on revealing that there was a baggie of cocaine hidden in the cleaning-supply closet," Miles answered, wondering what would happen if Ruth was ever cut off from her caffeine and sugar. "I verified it just now with the cop shop. Ortega said they found coke up there, but that it was a small amount."

Luis Ortega was a second-generation police officer, a detective now, and Miles's regular contact with the Flagstaff police. The two had been college roommates at the University of Northcentral Arizona, two years sharing a dorm room, and the last two in a house off campus. Miles knew that as a reporter he was lucky to have such a connection to local law enforcement, and he tried not to take advantage of that. Not that Luis would ever let him. But the two had settled into a comfortable working connection, not the adversarial norm for many reporter/law enforcement relationships. Flag PD had a revolving door of public information officers over the years, so Luis and the police department seemed good with Ortega being Miles's go-to when a big story broke, or even on background.

Miles told Ruth about Charlie's request, leaving out the fundraiser part. He noticed Lisha watching the exchange, poker-faced. She didn't even raise an eyebrow when he omitted that last bit.

"Walk with me," Ruth said as they left the break room in the back of the building and went toward the newsroom. The two reporters followed her, puppy-like, straining to keep up with her, despite her diminutive size.

"Are the police releasing the cocaine info?" Ruth asked, pausing in the middle of Advertising to take a swallow. She tapped today's metallic-blue fingernails on the cup.

"Turns out, they're not," Miles said. "So actually, if Charlie hadn't spilled the frijoles, knowing the police would eventually, we wouldn't be having this conversation."

"And when you say baggie, are we talking snack, sandwich, or let's-invite-the-neighborhood-over-for-a picnic sized container?"

"Probably the snack size," Miles said. "For personal use only, not a seller's amount. Less than a gram."

The three of them were in the newsroom now, and Ruth sat down at her desk, glancing at the computer screen, and then up at Lisha.

"What do you think?" Ruth asked her newest employee.

Lisha looked from Ruth to Miles, and back again.

"I'm new here, obviously, but I can see it from both sides," she started slowly. "When Charlie first asked this, I figured we'd ignore her request. But if it is really unrelated—and no other media outlets apparently have the information—then I could see waiting. Because we don't want to tie the two together if they aren't. You know, newspapers as gatekeepers, and all. But we should put it into a follow-up story soon."

"That's all?" Ruth asked.

"For now," Lisha answered.

"All right, since you two seem to be on the same page, let's sit on it for a day, two max. And tomorrow before you come in, Miles, swing by the observatory, and see if Charlie wants to add anything. Something seems off here. But do your regular cop-shop stop and sniff it out for any new developments. Lisha, you'll be doing copy editing with me tomorrow morning."

Miles and Lisha nodded.

"And while I understand your attempt at diplomacy, Lisha, don't ever put too much faith in another reporter's knowing better than you how to handle something. It doesn't matter that you're the newbie here. In fact, that can often lead to clarity of view."

"Okay," Lisha said.

Ruth motioned to the chair near hers.

"Now come sit for your next lesson on layout," Ruth said.

"Do you mind if I run to the bathroom first?"

Ruth laughed. "You don't need my permission for that."

"Right," Lisha said, smiling.

"See ya both tomorrow," Miles said.

But as he left through the outside door, Lisha was right behind him.

"Thanks for backing me up," Miles said.

"I'm concerned," Lisha said. "Honestly, the thing that makes me hesitate is the gift-shop kid using the word 'illegal.' If that's what he meant, you know, a cocaine connection, then it would be great if we scooped this. But if it's really a random thing, or he meant the cleaner was an undocumented worker, then I see why it's okay to hold that information."

"I have to admit something seems off with Charlie, but I can't put my finger on it."

"Yeah, it felt like she was sitting on something big—but I always feel my sources are withholding something from me," Lisha said, laughing. "And as a Black woman, I'm probably a bit suspicious of most white sources."

Miles wasn't sure if Lisha was joking or not. But he could tell she was going to be a good colleague.

"Good luck learning the editor ropes, Lisha."

Miles was almost home when his phone rang. Charlie told him she had an interview set up for him—now. He texted a quick update to Ruth and turned his bike toward Mars Hill.

Chapter 17

Miles stayed still while Feliciana Garcia wept silent tears. They sat in one of the observatory's conference rooms with Charlie. She had set up the interview with the dead woman's family, though it was just her sister who showed up. The woman turned to Miles now and shook her head.

"Who would do this?" she asked in a voice just above a whisper. He knew she did not expect any kind of answer. Then she took a big breath and squared her shoulders. "What do you want to know about my sister?"

"Anything you want to tell people. I know you said you were going to bury her in Mexico. I thought it would be nice to tell our readers what she was like," Miles explained. He kept his voice low and, he hoped, respectful. Over the years he had interviewed lots of people about their relatives or friends who had died. It was never easy, but he knew it was always easier for him than for them.

"What was she like?" he asked. "How long had she been visiting you?"

"Alejandra came north just last month," Feliciana told him. "She was ready for a new life in America. She stayed with our parents for years, taking care of them, and finally, now that they have passed, came to live with us."

Tears filled her eyes but did not spill onto her face.

"How can I make you see her? She was loving, she was funny, she had so many dreams for her life," she said. "She was a teacher in Mexico and hoped to be the same in the United States." She stopped talking and seemed to struggle to keep her composure.

Charlie gave Miles a look and patted Feliciana's arm.

"You don't have to say another word," Charlie said. "If this is all too much, you have no obligation to go on."

"That's exactly right," Miles added. "I'm sorry to have upset you."

"It is not *you* who has upset me," she said now, dabbing her tears with an embroidered handkerchief. "It is the person who killed her when she was just trying to live her life. Just getting started in this new place."

"Any reason you didn't report her disappearance right away?" he asked.

"She was staying at an apartment of a friend who was out of town," Feliciana said. "When she did not come over that next morning, we thought she was tired from working late. Then, when she did not come to work that second night, we became worried and went to check the apartment where she was staying just down the block from us."

Miles waited and was glad that Charlie did not interrupt. He thanked her years of working as a reporter for knowing when it was best to keep quiet.

"It is just that, normally it would have been my husband and me cleaning. If it had been the two of us, would someone have tried to kill us both? By her taking the shift that night, offering to do that work for us, that is what murdered her. And if I had been here by myself as I was so many nights, I would have known to be careful, and I would have fought back. Or else, it would be me dead in the woods, not my dear little sister."

She dropped her face into her hands and cried for real.

Charlie gave Miles another look, and he nodded. He closed his notebook and turned off the recorder, stowing them both in his sling bag.

"I am so, so sorry for your loss, Mrs. Garcia," he said.

"Thank you for asking me about my beloved sister," she said, raising her wet face out of her hands. "We will bury her at home next week, and I will tell my family that the community of Flagstaff noticed her passing when I lay flowers on her grave."

"I'll send Charlie a copy of the story, and she can get it to you before you leave. Do you have a picture you'd like me to put in the paper?"

Feliciana opened her purse and pulled out a well-worn photo of two small girls, their arms around each other, standing in front of a fenced-in donkey.

"This is the two of us at our grandfather's farm." She pointed to the smaller girl. "This is Alejandra. I believe she was six, and I was nine. She loved that little burro she called Pedro, and Grandfather used to tease her that she could always ride it into the sunset if life got too difficult. So I imagine her now, on her little Pedro, riding into the sunset to see our *abuelo* and *abuela*, and our parents."

"May I take this? I promise to get it back to you by tomorrow."

Feliciana looked fondly at the photograph, and then

handed it to Miles.

"It is the only photograph I have—in this country—of us. I am going to frame it."

So instead of taking it with him, Miles snapped a few shots of the photo with his *Gazette*-issued camera.

"Thank you," she said as she took the photo back and pressed it to her heart. With that, she walked out of the room with Charlie, and Miles gathered his things. Charlie came back in, looking angry.

"What?" he asked.

"I know you're going to write a nice story about her sister, but I hope you are sensitive to our reputation," she began.

Who had Charlie become? I hardly recognize her.

"Wait, what? You said it would be okay if I interviewed Alejandra's family. You set this up—which I really appreciate. So what's with the attitude?"

"The attitude? Is that what you call it?"

Miles could see that Charlie was upset, but he seriously had no idea why. And he thought he saw something else that wasn't right. Charlie's eyes looked glazed.

"Are you okay?" he asked, suddenly feeling real concern.

"Sorry, sorry. I will be when this is all over," she said, her mood flipping. "I'm under a lot of pressure here, and I gotta say this made it worse."

"What kind of pressure?" he asked, just as Beez opened the door and walked into the conference room.

"'Scuse the interruption, you two," he said. "But, Miles, your editor, Ruth is it, just called and asked you to get in touch. I guess she dialed your cell phone, but it was turned off. Didn't sound too happy about that."

Miles pulled out his phone, turned it back on, and saw he had three calls from his boss.

"Right. Gotta go. Let's talk later, Charlie."

He glided down the hill, wondering why Charlie was feeling pressured—and by whom.

Chapter 18

Maddy's new phone rang mid-morning as she was towel drying her hair. She felt a jolt shoot through her, but quickly reminded herself that Arthur did not have her new number. Spam already? Then she remembered two days earlier when she'd seen Miles Harper again at Caboose Coffee, he had offered to help her move and they had exchanged numbers.

"Hello," she said after making sure the caller did not have a Wisconsin area code. Arthur was an excellent hunter, she knew.

"Hiya, Madeline."

"Good morning, Miles."

"So I've finished with my mental workout for the day, and now need a physical challenge. You wanna help me out with that? I'm ready to move some boxes."

Maddy smiled. She had all but decided to do it on her own, but with his sweet approach and her growing sense of isolation in a new town, why would she say no? Just shy of a month into her new life, and perhaps she had found one friend.

"That would be wonderful. If you want to come over to the MoMo in a half hour, I will be ready."

"The MoMo? Don't think I know it."

"Oh, sorry. The Mountain Motel on Route 66, just east of where that road cuts over the tracks—Enterprise Street, I think?"

"Enterprise Drive. Okay, I know that place. You'll have to fill me in on the nickname."

"Sure, and thanks. I will take you to lunch afterward."

"Sounds great."

After hanging up, Maddy put on jeans, her new long-sleeved Dark Skies Flagstaff T-shirt, a denim work shirt, and pulled on her Converse, which she had not worn in probably three years. The sky-blue shoes had been lost in her closet and in her mind, behind the several pairs of high heels that Arthur had bought her. The sneakers were pure cozy.

Daisy was lying on her side, eyes closed, legs twitching.

"Go get that squirrel, girl," Maddy whispered. They had hiked for an hour up the path behind the MoMo that morning, and several of those squirrels with the gigantic ears had made it their business to tease Daisy from high above, one scampering down the ponderosa pine trunks and chattering, just a dog-nose length away.

Maddy put two twenties on the bedside table, and then added one more. The maids had come just once a week as she requested, so she did not think she needed to tip any more than that. She took a last look around the room that her been her home for the past month. She picked up her suitcases, put on her backpack, and headed out, closing the door before Daisy could join her. She loaded the stuff into her rental car and walked back up for a box of things she had accumulated since her arrival. This time on the way down Daisy trotted beside her, the dream squirrel temporarily forgotten. After putting the last box into the car, she went to the front office to say goodbye.

Karan smiled as they walked in.

"This is our sad morning, is it not, Miss Maddy and Daisy?" he asked, his face all smiles but his voice somber.

"Yes it is, Karan," she said, returning the smile. "But I will still be in town, and I can drop by from time to time."

"I do hope you do that. You have made quite a positive impression on my entire family."

"Oh?" Maddy was surprised. She had only said hello to Urvi a couple of times, and except for the first meeting with Tanak and Amita, it was mostly Karan with whom she communicated.

"You may be surprised, but we get many guests who act like we are not human," he explained, the unlit cigarette working 'round and 'round his fingertips. "They check in without getting off their cell phones, they call down angry about something wrong in their rooms—often an issue which they themselves have caused—they hardly say hello when interacting with us, and then they leave the rooms entirely untidy."

"Oh, I had no idea."

"I do not mean to share my complaints with you, but only want to say that all of us have appreciated your kindness. No, your humanness."

"And I appreciate you, all of you, too. You really helped me feel welcome during a difficult time," she said, then rushed to safer ground. "Here's my key, and of course I tried to leave my room in good shape."

"I have no doubt."

Tanak walked in through the back door, saw Maddy, and turned away.

"Can you say hello to Miss Maddy," Karan said, echoing the words Tanak himself had said to his sister in what felt like a long time ago. "She is leaving us today."

Tan looked at Maddy then and seemed to force a smile.

"Good luck to you, Miss Maddy," he said, kneeling down in front of Daisy. "You, too, happy doggy. Take care of your mama."

Maddy felt unexpected tears sting her eyes.

"Thank you, Tan," she said. But he was already out the door.

"How is he doing, Karan?" she asked quietly.

"About the same, I would say. But his mother and I are taking both of our children out to dine tonight. We thought they might be a bit more open if we are away from here and home and eating together in a new setting."

Maddy saw Miles ride up to the office on his bicycle, an orange one this time.

"Sounds like a good plan, Karan. Good luck. And here's my helper."

Miles leaned his bike on a wall, walked into the office, and Maddy introduced the two men. Daisy trotted over to Miles to collect a few pats.

"How long you owned the motel?" Miles asked.

"It's been five years this month," he said. "We moved here from India to purchase it from cousins who moved back home. They bought it from the long-time owners about five years before that."

Karan came out from behind the counter and called Daisy, who left Miles for the man with the treat.

"Good girl, Daisy. Now as Tanak said, you take

good care of Miss Maddy, will you?"

The dog's tail wagged, and she licked Karan on his chin.

"Would you like to leave a forwarding address?" Karan asked, standing back up, wiping his chin with a handkerchief.

"Probably not," she said, suddenly wishing Miles had stayed outside. "Miles, would you mind putting Daisy in the car? It's that white Ford Explorer."

"Sure. Good to meet you, Karan," he said, walking out with the dog.

Maddy turned back to Karan.

"I appreciate how you offered to keep my stay private, and I would not want you to even know my new address, in case somehow someone got hold of it," she said.

"I understand completely. Now you go, and do come back and see us. I want to see your new car when you get one. Your wheels, is that not the expression?"

"Yes," Maddy said. "I plan on getting one soon, maybe even next week. And I will put the motel review online, only anonymously, okay?"

"Fabuloso, Miss Maddy."

"Fabuloso, Karan."

She gave him a quick hug, which he reciprocated lightly. She felt the tickle of tears threatening again and walked quickly out the door.

She and Miles decided he would ride his bike to her new abode and meet her there. She lost sight of him in her rearview mirror and was surprised to find him, less than ten minutes later, sitting on the steps of her tiny porch beyond a small patio, the bike propped up on an aspen tree.

“How in the world did you beat me here?” she asked.

“Bikes can go places cars can’t,” he said, obviously trying to look like he wasn’t breathing hard. He glanced around. “This is a great neighborhood. Close to the little Dashas’, the urban trail, and downtown—the heart of Flagstaff. You scored.”

“The little Dashas?”

“The Dashas’ grocery store named after Fred Dasha, a former candidate for governor who ran the company, was on all these boards of education and stuff. I interviewed him maybe a decade after he ran for governor—and lost. It was a story on state politics. He seemed really genuine about helping others. Anyway, the store is just down the hill from here. Maybe five blocks? They had a fire a few years ago, and locals were concerned they’d just shut it down. But when they reopened, they’d added a health-food section. Not giant, but decent. There’s a larger Dashas’ near the UNA campus.”

“You like to cook?”

“Love cooking, which is lucky ’cause I love eating,” he said with his lopsided grin. “You?”

“I enjoy food, but nothing like a full-fledged foodie. I’d say you sound like one.”

“Not sure about that.”

Maddy stepped around a bucket of soapy water and a squeegee and opened the front door.

“Your landlord has high cleaning standards,” he said, nodding at the bucket. “A good sign.”

“Landlady.”

“Landlady, sorry,” Miles said, and he followed her inside, Daisy the caboose. Miles appeared speechless for the first time since they had met. Not for that long, though.

"You totally scored, Madeline," he whispered.

"Great place, yes?" Maddy said and then gasped and clapped her hands. "Fresh daisies!"

Miles grinned at her joy, the dog looked up expectantly, and the humans laughed.

"Her name is Ethel, and we really hit if off last week," Maddy said. "She met Daisy, too, so I bet that choice of flowers is no coincidence."

Afternoon light flooded through sparkling bay windows, showing off the cream-colored and one brick-red wall. A rust and blue Navajo rug covered a third of the hardwood floor, and a built-in wooden hutch held china and glasses. In one corner was a stuffed chair and loveseat, both covered in a cloth of dark navy adorned with tiny red diamond shapes, with carved wooden feet below. A painting of a cluster of piñon trees in front of the Grand Canyon hung over the couch. A round oak table, surrounded by four wooden chairs, held the blue glass pitcher of fresh daisies.

Behind the living room was a small kitchen with wooden cabinets, a porcelain sink, and stainless-steel refrigerator and stove. The floor was terracotta tile.

Miles whistled, and Daisy looked up again.

"This place is just so beautiful," he said quietly.

"I know. Here, let me show you the rest, and then we can unload."

He followed her into a small bedroom-turned-office painted a light blue, with a window, couch, and wooden desk. Then on to a slightly larger bedroom, painted a soothing light green with two corner windows dressed in lace curtains, a double bed, wooden dresser, tall bookshelf, tiny dressing table and chair, and another Navajo rug. A watercolor of night-time Flagstaff hung over the bed.

"Hey, that's the view from Mars Hill," Miles exclaimed. "On the road up to the observatory." He didn't tell her it's where teenagers and college kids went to make out at night, and more. Or so rumors had it.

"Is it? Then, here is what really hooked me."

She walked into a medium-sized bathroom, whose shower walls were covered in turquoise tiles.

"This kind of feels like my grandmother's house back in Illinois," Miles said. "Old school."

Maddy blanched but turned away before Miles could register her expression. She'd nearly blocked out that he was from the Midwest, too. She'd have to remember. But she swallowed her feelings and walked back into the living room. Chicago and Milwaukee were close in proximity, but actually worlds apart. And Arthur's reach would not have a hold on this random guy. Even to think it showed Maddy how nuts she had become since the marriage. She banished her thoughts, something she seemed to be doing more and more these days.

"And here is what Daisy loves the most," she said, crossing the kitchen and opening the back door. The dog trotted out to a small yard, circled around twice, and flopped down beneath one of the two fruit trees.

"Apple trees?" Miles asked.

"One apple and one red pear," she said. "Ethel, my landlady, lives in the front house, and said I could help myself to any, as long as they're from the top, where she can no longer reach. She's got a ladder but promised her son she would not climb up anymore."

"She older?"

"Probably in her late seventies, I would say. She said her husband, who died some years ago, built her house in the '50s, and this little one as a getaway for her in the '60s. She's been living in the big house since she was a new bride, as she put it. They named the little house their casita, after having spent some winters down in Mexico. You should see her garden. It is just around that gate. But she is a bit of a talker, so I would like to get moved in before you meet her."

"Right."

They went out to the Explorer for the suitcases, backpack, dog bed, and a box. Miles reached for the box, but she stopped him.

"Let me get that one, Miles. Would you grab the suitcases?"

"No worries," he said, holding onto the box, which was heavy. "I just thought—"

"Please," she said, cutting him off. "I will take the box."

"Sure, okay."

As he followed her inside, holding the suitcases and feeling the ribs tingle from his slide down Mount Elden, he scratched his head mentally. Maybe she was insulted that he assumed he was stronger than she? But it was not as if the suitcases were canary feathers. It was her moving day, though, and he let it go.

They put all the belongings into the study, Maddy putting the box on the desk and resting the backpack on top of that.

"To the FedEx?" she said, sounding upbeat again.

There they would pick up more boxes she had

mailed to herself last month. They drove onto Milton Road, turned onto Plaza Way, and collected a half dozen more boxes. There were so many items from her married years she had left behind. But Maddy knew she had everything she needed for now, for her new life.

Chapter 19

Rafat Shukla's head bobbed to Drake's "Take Care," on his iPod, white wires spilling from his ears as he vacuumed a room at the Mountain Motel.

There was something about rap, and especially Drake. A Canadian-born rapper, his lyrics always got to Rafat. They weren't as dark as some other rappers, and they were smart. Plus, he sang and rapped all at once, which was different, too.

Rafat was a rapper, and one day he hoped to make it big. His mother despised it because she said rap and hip-hop were too violent and dark. But he would write songs she'd be proud of.

His mother was a distant cousin of Karan and Urvi Vohra. Rafat had grown up in Los Angeles but moved to Arizona with his mom to get away from the gang influences, first in Phoenix, and now in Flagstaff. He'd never told his mother, but he was relieved to get out of the cities, where he knew he would have had to join a gang to survive. There were some wannabe gangs in Flagstaff, sure, but nobody had leaned on him yet, thank the gods. He was done with all that. He'd never killed anybody, but he had snitched on a couple of people for one of the neighborhood gangs, and then ignored what might have happened to those guys. This place was boring, sure, but he could actually breathe here. He also discovered that writing songs was a lot easier when you weren't afraid all the time.

The only thing that bothered him in this new place was that he was expected to be best friends with his cousin, Tanak. The kid was a head case. Sometimes friendly, sometimes acting like he didn't even know Rafat. Then, the other night, he saw Tanak in the motel parking lot talking to some guy who looked like no good. His eyes were flat-out scary. Ice on ice. Rafat wanted to warn the kid to stay away from thugs. He just didn't know how to convey the message in a way Tanak would appreciate—or listen. He'd always heard from his mom that Tanak and his sister Amita were the goodie-goodie types, but now he wasn't so sure. Didn't seem like that, these past few weeks when it came to his boy cousin. That one night, from the cleaning closet just above the parking lot where he'd gone to retrieve a mop and bucket, he'd overheard Tanak talking to the man. Tanak had called the guy Frank-man. What kind of name was that? Should he say something to his mother or his aunt and uncle? He decided he'd wait. It really wasn't his business.

The Mountain Motel was one of about a dozen Flagstaff motels owned by east Indians—as opposed to American Indians who, from where Rafat sat, didn't own squat. He didn't mind cleaning to help out his mother in covering their rent, even if it was way reduced by Karan.

Rafat paused in his cleaning, stepped outside, and pulled out his golden fountain pen, a birthday present from his mother. That was the advantage to night cleaning. He could always stop to capture a couple of lines. He couldn't be certain, but it felt like his songs were getting stronger.

Night sky, tight sky
everything all right sky,
soon no moon,
babe, let's croon.

Maybe spoon? Both old-fashioned words—which his mom would appreciate, haha.

He was about to start another verse, but before he could write "Light sky," he saw a flash of something in his peripheral vision, something shining in the dusty moonlight.

"No!" he thought, turning to face the assailant, Rafat's pen extended like a weapon.

The knife cut into him before he could lunge. It struck again and again. The young man was dead before he hit the ground, notebook clenched in his hand. His cherished fountain pen rolled quietly away from his body, as steps retreated.

Chapter 20

Maddy drove her new Subaru Outback Sport—an almost SUV—toward the MoMo. She wanted to say hello to Karan, tell him about her baking job, and show off her new wheels. He had teased her that a woman without a car was like a child without a sibling in his native India. She knew he would be happy for her. She also wanted to see how Tanak was doing. *The Prize.*

It was getting colder in Flagstaff since her arrival some five weeks ago. This morning had been 22 degrees, for gosh sake. But sunny, unlike the many overcast November days in Wisconsin. Daisy's head hung out of the back window, tongue long as she gulped the air after their late-afternoon five-mile run. Well, Maddy's five miles to probably Daisy's eight, ten, off leash. She braked hurriedly as she saw two police cars blocking the motel's lobby entrance. Yellow crime tape waved in the low breeze. She pulled over in a parking lot next door and jogged to the motel.

"Can't go in there, miss," a police officer told her. "It's a crime scene. You're going to have to find a different motel to stay at."

"No, no. I am not looking for a motel. I am a friend of the Vohras."

She saw Karan and Urvi sitting inside the lobby, slumped in their chairs. Karan looked up, saw Maddy, and slowly got up and walked outside.

"It is all right, officer. We know Miss Maddy. She was our guest for a month."

Karan's voice was hushed, his eyes rimmed in pink.

The officer stepped aside, but not far.

"What happened? Is your family okay? Your kids?"

"We had a very sad death, Miss Maddy," he said.

"A guest?" Maddy asked, hoping it was a heart attack or something else natural. *But then why would this be a crime scene? Of course, it would not be.*

"Our cousin's son Rafat, he died of what sounds like knife wounds," he said, making no eye contact. Urvi walked out and took her husband's arm in hers.

"Hello, Miss Maddy," she said quietly. "Karan, we need to go back inside and wait for the children."

"Is there anything I can do?" Maddy asked.

"Nothing," he said. "The police are talking to Tanak. He was the one who found the body and has blood all over him from trying to revive his cousin. His sister is being driven home from school. Oh, here she is."

Karan and Urvi turned to greet Amita, who ran into their arms. The three walked back into the lobby without another word.

Chapter 21

Miles finished filing his latest story and pedaled to the carwash/gas station on Milton Road. The coffee there was strong and cheap, and when Miles saw all the pumps were filled and cars were lined up waiting, he gave himself a mental pat for being a bike-only guy. As he locked up his ride, he found himself imagining Madeline and him on a bike ride and ending up on a blanket in the woods, her face flushed above him.

Whoa, quit! Where the hell did that come from? he chided himself. He hardly knew her, for God's sake. He straightened up and looked around, forcing himself back to reality.

A driver of a shuttle van that took up two pumps because of the attached luggage trailer left the van in place as he walked toward the store. A woman in a station wagon with a couple of kids leaned out her window at him.

"*Hola*, would you move your vehicles before you go inside, please?" she called out.

The driver looked at her but kept on walking toward the gas-station store without a word. Tall and thin, with thick glasses, the guy looked familiar.

She leaned on the horn, and as Miles followed the driver inside, the guy raised his middle finger at the woman without looking back. He pushed opened the door and walked in. Miles heard the woman yelling something in Spanish just before the door closed behind him.

Inside, Miles filled up his metal “Don’t PHX FLG” to-go cup at the coffee pot, grabbed a copy of *The Arizona Republic,* and stood in line. The cup’s words were some Flagstaff locals’ expression of hope to keep their town from becoming an asphalt jungle like the state capitol. His plan: enjoy a cup of coffee, read the Phoenix newspaper, and check in with Ruth on what he’d filed. This afternoon, he’d get an update from Luis on the murder investigation.

The shuttle driver stood behind him, holding a couple of bags of corn nuts and sticks of beef jerky. The door dinged, and the station-wagon woman put her head in.

“Señor, would you please move your van so we can purchase some gas?” she asked, nodding toward the waiting cars. “My kids are having fits.”

The van driver kept his back to her. But Miles heard him say, “Stupid bitch,” under his breath.

“Hey, you mind moving the shuttle and paying after?” asked the young man behind the counter. A Navajo, he was sporting a long ponytail and a turquoise choker.

“I do mind. I’ll move it after I get my cigs,” said the man, whose nametag read, “Stan”.

Snap! Miles remembered. Stan had been at the SB 1070 protest—protesting the protesters. Miles moved aside.

“Hey, man,” he said neutrally. “Go ahead. I’m in no hurry.”

The shuttle driver did not seem to recognize Miles.

The woman walked outside, letting the door slam

behind her.

Stan gave Miles a "just us bros" smile, and then turned his attention to the wall of cigarettes behind the counter.

"Gimme two packs of Marlboro Golds," he said.

The clerk unlocked the plastic case and handed him the cigarettes.

"Sorry about that. It's just that the line's building up," he said. "It can get crazy out there."

The guy looked at the kid.

"That ain't my problem, buddy."

He walked out with his hands clenched. Outside, he tore open one of the packs, tapped out a cigarette, and lit it, ignoring honks of a couple of vehicles. He took a few long puffs, blew out the smoke, then stomped the cigarette out on the pavement. He climbed back into the van and drove off, giving what seemed a mocking tap on the horn as he exited. Miles wondered how someone working for the shuttle company that drove passengers back and forth from Flagstaff to the Phoenix airport could have such a rotten demeanor.

"You get it coming and going dontcha?" Miles asked the clerk, whose arm displayed a raven tattoo.

"You don't know the half of it. Bet I'll get an earful from the station-wagon mom, too."

"Maybe she'll pay at the pump?" Miles offered.

"Hopefully," the kid said.

He did not sound hopeful. Not one bit.

Chapter 22

After a couple of hours of cleaning his workspace earlier that week, Miles had seen glimpses of his actual desktop. En route to a clean surface, he had discovered something hiding under the mountain of papers. A Styrofoam container from the enchilada sale that had been, when? Maybe it was a month or two ago when two women from Circulation came through the newsroom offering their delicious homemade enchiladas to raise money for some high school team. But it wasn't just the box that was hidden. In the box were the half dozen enchiladas. They were green, even though he was pretty sure he had ordered the red chile. No wonder his corner of the newsroom had been a bit ripe. Very ripe. Damn it.

Ruth and Cawdry caught him tossing the greasy take-home box into the wastebasket and showed no mercy.

"Hoarders are losers. Food hoarders are sickos," Ruth yelled across the desks.

Cawdry put his head down on his own desk, unable to say a thing through his gasps of laughter.

But then Miles's phone beeped and took him to Instagram. There was a post—from Cawdry—showing the whole world Miles's mess of a desk, the second photo of the enchiladas in the wastebasket. "Newsman too busy to eat mold!" read the caption.

"Thanks, Cawdry," Miles said sarcastically.

"Too great an image not to post, man."

Miles shook his head, but then compared the Instagram image to his current desk. Well, if nothing else, it proved he was getting it cleaned up. And who cared if he had a messy desk anyway? Not as bad as Cawdry's mess-up from last year. The university sports teams were called the Lumberjacks, and the women teams were the Lady Jacks. The headline, after the soccer women's first game of the season, even made it onto the Ellen DeGeneres' bloopers report.

"Lady Jacks off to a good start."

Miles would have loved to Tweet that out into the world and tag Cawdry's name, but it would have reflected badly on the newspaper, and gotten the sports guy fired. Not to mention that Miles would have lost his job, too. Still, he smiled as he imagined putting it out there. Now all the women's teams were simply called the Lumberjacks, like the men.

Miles was startled, because Ruth was standing right next to his desk chair. She hardly ever came over to this side of the newsroom.

"Miles, listen. If you clean up your act, you'll become more organized, and that usually means a better journalist," she said in a rare, quiet voice. "Honestly, I've seen more than one brilliant reporter's career go down the drain because their disorganization or ADHD or whatever they called it would not let them see clearly. I don't want you to go down that way."

And then she was gone. It was the only time he'd heard Ruth say something in hushed tones, let alone something that was so supportive. He blinked in surprise.

"I mean it, Harper. Get the hell to work and move it on the cleaning!" she yelled across the newsroom again, as if to cover up her apparent concern for him.

"On it!" he called back.

Okay, okay, I'll clean up my act, he told himself. If he could be a better reporter, smarter journalist, by being tidier—which should breed better organization—he was all in. He suddenly flashed on the fact that he'd been a very organized kid, almost a neatnik, but his older sister had been a major slob. Could he have subconsciously taken up that part of her identity after she died?

He was putting the last stray papers into a file when Lisha came in, reporting for her editing shift. His phone rang; he grabbed it, and noticed he didn't have to dig through papers to locate it. It was Luis.

"Big story coming in," Miles announced to the newsroom. He listened some more to Ortega, and then hung up. He grabbed his jacket off the back of his chair, nodded to Lisha to follow him. Lisha hesitated, looking at their boss.

"Got another body," he said. "Will call from the scene." He shoved his phone into its obnoxious holder, Ruth waved them out the door, and they took off.

"I'll drive," Lisha said. "Where to?"

"The MoMo."

"Where?"

"The Mountain Motel on Route 66. A friend of mine calls it the MoMo," he said. What a relief that Madeline no longer lived there. He wondered who could have been killed. And was it the same perpetrator?

He'd barely clicked his seat belt when the Volvo

surged forward.

"I love speed," Lisha said, smiling at his look of surprise. "Growing up, my family only owned beaters that had to be jump-started on a regular basis. I got this bad baby a makeover after I bought her—a fully rebuilt engine."

"I'll talk to the cops," Miles suggested, trying to ignore the flip of his stomach from Lisha's driving. "And let's both see if we can get any witnesses to talk to us. Sound okay?"

Lisha nodded, and they were there. She pulled up at the MoMo in a lot less time than they would have made it in most cars, not to mention on two wheels.

Chapter 23

Yellow police tape stretched across the driveway of the Mountain Motel fluttered in the breeze. A young police officer stood out front, arms folded over his chest, looking bored.

"What happened here, officer?" asked a man passing by, holding a plastic grocery bag.

Two joggers slowed as well, running in place to hear the cop's response.

"Okay, folks. You should move along now. It's a crime scene, is all I can tell you."

The runners took off, but then stopped and hovered in front of the business next door to the motel.

"Course, sorry to bother you," said Groceries.

"Not a problem," answered the officer, and he nodded at the joggers to keep moving.

"But what the hell is happening to our small, friendly town?" Groceries asked, and then walked away.

The officer heard his supervisor's voice click on over his radio.

"Would you keep the lookie-Lous out of here?" Luis Ortega asked.

"Ten-four, sir."

"But before you kick them out, get the ID of anyone hanging around."

"Ten-four."

The three watchers were already gone, though. The cop, born and raised in Flagstaff, had only been with department for three months after leaving the Phoenix police. Most people started in Flagstaff and moved on and up. But officer Hank Percy could not stand the big city—the noise, the traffic, the inability to connect with people—where he served for barely two years. Now as he watched Joggers and Groceries from a distance, he thought about that guy's question.

Just what was *happening to his small, friendly town?*

Chapter 24

Maddy was walking to her new car when she heard a familiar voice.

"Madeline! What's going on?" Miles asked.

He was standing just outside the police tape, pulling his audio recorder out of his pack.

"Do not turn that on, please," she said.

"Okay," he said, shoving it back into his bag. "What's happened here?"

Maddy hesitated. She did not want to tell him that Tanak was being questioned. Miles had met Karan the one time but would not feel any loyalty to the kid. He was a journalist first and fully.

"You will need to ask the police, Miles," she said. "I just got here to show Karan my new car and found all this."

"Would you just tell me Karan's wife's name?" he asked, nodding toward the vestibule windows. "That's her inside, right?"

"Yes. Urvi—U-R-V-I. And Karan has two As. Now that's it, Miles. I mean it."

She suddenly felt both drained and irritated.

Miles walked with her to the car, seemingly oblivious to her mood.

"Wow, a Subarubie. Cool," he said with his now-familiar lopsided grin.

She felt herself thawing. He was not the bad guy

here.

“Maybe you will get a ride someday,” she said, turning to open the driver’s door. “The color is Newport Blue Pearl, and her name is Pearl.”

“I like the silver highlights,” Miles said.

Luis Ortega walked over. Miles introduced them before Maddy could open the door.

“My officer said you were staying here at the motel, Ms. Sullivan. When?” Ortega asked.

“Up until a week or ten days or so ago? I stayed here for a month. They were so good to me,” she added, her eyes filling with tears. She felt the detective’s intense gaze.

“Give us some privacy, Miles?” Ortega asked, more a command than a question. He waited for Miles to move out of earshot.

“We will need to interview you,” Ortega told Maddy. “I would appreciate it if you would come into the office tomorrow.” He handed her his card. “And what is your contact information?”

She gave him her phone number and Ethel’s address and turned to go.

“Please do not leave Flagstaff until we talk with you,” Ortega said.

“Oh,” she answered, surprised. “I am not planning on going anywhere.”

“Where do you work?”

“Caboose Coffee bakery. I am just starting,” she said. “Working late nights.”

She noticed Miles easing his way back toward them. Ortega caught her glance and turned to Miles, who tried but failed to look nonchalant as he turned away.

"You are free to go now, Ms. Sullivan," Ortega said. "I hope to see you tomorrow. Are you okay to drive? You seem shaken. Shall I have one of my officers give you a ride?"

"I think I am okay, thank you, Detective," she said, taking a big breath. "I am headed home now—just a few blocks away. My dog is in the car."

"Drive carefully. Especially if that's a new vehicle," Ortega said.

Maddy felt a chill move through her—had he been watching her movements in this little town? Was he aligned with Arthur? Then she saw the obvious paper license plate that indicated a new car and once again reproached herself for her instant suspicions of men. She had not been like that before Arthur. Had she?

She climbed into Pearl and drove away from the MoMo without saying another word to the detective or Miles. She glimpsed the two of them in her side mirror. They stood on the parking lot together, having what looked like an intense conversation.

She parked in the driveway of her new home, deep in thought. Karan had said the police were interviewing Tan because he had found the body. But if he had blood on his clothing, could it be something else? Of course, it could. Her hand on the door handle, she felt Daisy lick the back of her neck.

"Okay, okay, we are getting out," she said, but still sat there.

No way. She had met the kid. Tan may have been silent lately with his parents, but she could absolutely not imagine him as a killer. She wanted to talk to Miles about it but did not yet trust him to keep something like this to himself. What would she tell Ortega tomorrow?

She finally opened the door and walked inside, Daisy beside her. She would take a bath, make supper, and figure it all out. A glass of wine might be called for, except that she'd not purchased any alcohol since she arrived in Flagstaff. Tonight just might be the night to do so, but her cozy casita was awaiting.

Just before she was about to close her door to the outside world, she heard the "yoo-hoo" of her landlady. At first she felt irritated, even harassed, her privacy invaded. She needed time alone. But then it hit her. Who else would be better to talk with than her landlady and neighbor, who had no connection to the press or to law enforcement? Plus, she liked Ethel, and the woman was a good listener. Maybe she might even have some insight. Probably.

She returned the "yoo-hoo."

Chapter 25

"I was about to pour myself a libation," Ethel Naderman said. "Would you care to join me?"

The elderly woman wore a wide-brimmed bonnet, the knees of her loose jeans were covered in dirt, and her smile was as wide as her hat. "After I wash up, of course. And I also need to clean up after the man I *hired* to clean up." She laughed, nodding toward the piles of weeds on the sidewalk.

"I would love to join you. But may I help?"

"Oh, no thank you. I can do it in a jiffy," Ethel said. "Shall we meet in my yard in, say, fifteen minutes?"

"I'd like that," Maddy said, surprising herself at how strongly she meant it.

"Do you like G&T's?"

"Sounds perfect," Maddy said. "I can bring cheese and crackers."

After feeding Daisy and taking a quick shower, Maddy pulled on jeans and a light blue turtleneck, and went to the kitchen. She cut slices of Granny Smith apples, Jarlsberg cheese, and pulled some Ak-mak crackers out of the box. She grabbed brown mustard and two small plates. She walked over to Ethel's yard, carrying the food and holding the newspaper under one arm and black jean jacket over her other arm. She noted the piles of weeds were gone. She put the plates and snacks onto the patio table and waited for her hostess. It was a horseshoe-shaped yard, in which a grassy area met a garden that held faded roses and cosmos, lovely but no longer fragrant. Daisy got busy inspecting the yard with her nose.

Maddy felt sadness about the killing, yet a growing sense of safety and contentment at having landed here—in Flagstaff and at Ethel's. The older woman returned, carrying a tray of assorted bottles and glasses. Maddy jumped up to take it from her. The two women settled into the wooden chairs, on flowered pillows. Ethel handed Maddy a glass of bubbling tonic.

"Help yourself to the gin. I was not sure how strong you liked them. That is a two-ounce jigger. It is copper and from Mexico."

Maddy poured a jigger's worth into her glass, and then added one of the lime wedges.

"G&T's are my favorite summer drink, but since we are experiencing Indian summer, I thought I would make them," Ethel said. "I know I should not use that expression anymore, but I grew up with it, and never thought of it as any prejudice against Native Americans. I can see how it is a slight, though, so I should just say, 'our extended summer,' I suppose. Anyway, here's to a few more warm nights before we become socked in for the winter."

"Hear, hear," Maddy said. She clinked her crystal glass to Ethel's and took a sip.

"Oh, delicious," she said.

"Thank you, Madeline," Ethel said, and then turned her gaze toward her tenant. "Now, would you like to talk about it?"

"About?"

"About whatever has you upset. Pain is written all over your face. You do not have to share, of course. But I am here to listen if you want to talk."

Ethel helped herself to the fruit and cheese and crackers, and Maddy did the same, gathering her thoughts and emotions.

"You know the Vohras, the family at the Mountain Motel where I stayed before I found you?" Maddy asked.

"You said they were a wonderful family."

"There was a murder at the motel today, or maybe last night, and one of their cousins was killed. I just stopped by there, and the police were everywhere. He was stabbed to death, sounds like."

"Oh my gracious. I am so sorry," Ethel said. "Two murders in one month's time. I cannot fathom that here in Flagstaff."

"It is terrible. I feel so badly for that family. And then this detective acted all suspicious of me, and I have to go for an interview at the police station," she said. "I know it makes sense. I mean, I stayed there, and I am new to town, and the observatory murder happened around the time I arrived. But it's still, I am not sure why, but it makes me feel vulnerable, I suppose. I wanted to keep my head down and not expose myself much."

Ethel leaned over and patted her hand.

"Would you like me to come along as, say, a character witness? No way are you a perp! At my age, people tend to either act as if I were invisible or see me as full of wisdom. I am certain I could play the wise-one role for you with that detective."

"Oh, thank you, but that is all right. It is not as if

you know me all that well yet either," Maddy said. She smiled. "Based on your choice of words, though, I am guessing you are a mystery lover?"

"I am mad for them, it is true. I have read crime novels for years, and am helplessly addicted to the PBS mystery series," she said. "My husband Jer would watch with me, but he was more a nonfiction guy. That man adored *Nova*."

"I love PBS *Mystery*, too" Maddy said.

They sipped their drinks and nibbled in silence for a few minutes. Maddy broke the ice.

"You must think it's strange that I want to stay under the wire," she said slowly.

"It is not my business. And anyway, everyone has a different level of comfort in socializing—from extreme introverts to the most boisterous extroverts," she said. "I was an introvert married to an extrovert. But I came out of my shell over the years with my hon."

"I was married too," Maddy said quietly. "I used to be an extrovert, but I kind of got that kicked out of me."

Maddy surprised herself. She did not know Ethel well, but, then again, there was something safe about her, something comforting.

"I am so sorry, dear."

"I do not need to share the details, but he was a real Don Juan before we married—calling all the time, sending me flowers, buying me things. I was seriously swept off my feet," she said. "I know that sounds superficial of me. After we married, most of the first year was great. But after that, he became darker and darker and started accusing me of all kinds of things—how I was no longer playing the role of devoted wife. How I was cheating on him with anybody I ever talked to. Men and women."

"Oh, my."

"Then, well, I will just say it went beyond angry words."

"Oh, Madeline. I am so sorry," Ethel repeated. "Nobody deserves that. Until a few years ago, I was a volunteer for Flagstaff Victim Services—a support group here in town. I heard so many ugly stories. Horrible."

Maddy nodded.

"It's bizarre because as a graphic designer, for one project I did interviews with women who had been abused. I spent a lot of time with these victims to get to know the halfway house that had hired me to put together a brochure and webpage. But I could not see it in myself until he was, well, until it was too late."

"Too late?"

"Not too late for me, but too late for our marriage," Maddy said quickly. "Coming out west was, I suppose, my first move toward my well-being."

She felt she could tell Ethel more, much more, but suddenly did not have the energy.

"That is a mighty courageous step of self-care," Ethel said.

"Anyway, I feel like I am on a new path—and Flagstaff, and you and your house, and even the MoMo are all part of that."

"I understand, dear. And let me just say that, even though you spent time with those women who had been trapped in bad relationships, we never really look at ourselves the same way we look at strangers, do we? So I urge you not to be hard on yourself. From what I learned during that work, many of these abusive, often narcissistic, men—and there are some abusive women, too, though fewer—are incredibly charming in the initial stages. Like those pedophile groomers, except they are not preying on children."

"I had not thought of it that way, Ethel. Thank you."

Then she switched topics, reporting the scene at the motel and about running into Miles.

"The reporter who helped you move in?" Ethel asked.

This septuagenarian did not miss a thing, Maddy realized.

"Yes. I met him at Caboose Coffee shop my first week here."

"It is good to make friends you can trust," Ethel said.

Maddy felt a stab of regret about Belinda. *Was she still in California?* She *had* to call her soon. Tomorrow. She was starting to remind herself of Scarlett O'Hara.

"True. What about you, Ethel? Who do you spend time with in Flagstaff? I think you told me earlier you have a son. Is that right?"

"Brad. He and his wife live in Albuquerque. I have a few women friends, but most of them have moved away to get away from the winters and the altitude."

"That sounds tough."

"Brad and his wife do not drive over much. You know, busy with their careers. He and Jer were closer than we were all along. I suppose I was the, how do they say it, the bad cop? Jer was the lenient one, and so as a younger woman, a mom, I somehow felt I needed to counteract that. I did not know until after he passed that Brad and I were no longer very connected to one another. I have tried to reach out, but, well, as I said, he is busy."

"That's tough," Maddy said again. "I wonder if you are both still grieving—your husband, his father."

"I suppose so. But he seems more interested in seeing me move out of my house and into a retirement community than anything else," she said. "I suppose eventually that will happen. But I love my home."

"Well, until it does, I will be here for you, Ethel."

"You could do me one favor," Ethel said, a gleam in her eye.

"Sure. Anything."

"If Brad ever comes by and asks how I am faring, please say 'wonderfully!' And if you ever have concerns about my health—or state of mind, for that matter—come to me first."

"Deal," Maddy said.

"I have been wondering how you got your name. Madeline is a bit old fashioned for your generation."

"My aunt was named after the Madeline books, and I was named after my aunt, so I suppose I was named after the smallest—Madeline," Maddy said.

"Oh, yes."

Ethel began to recite the words about the twelve little girls in two straight lines who live in an old vine-covered house in Paris, and Maddy joined her, word for word.

The two women smiled at each other, and continued, finishing the recitation with the smallest girl being Madeline.

"Ludwig Bemelmans, an Austrian," Ethel said, and Maddy nodded.

"I see you're reading our local paper," Ethel said,

tipping her chin toward the *Gazette.*

"A bit thin?" Maddy said.

"And keeps getting thinner," Ethel said. "Recently they cut out the Monday paper altogether. Most of the subscribers read the online version, and it is just old folks like me who still get it plopped down on our driveways. Subscriptions are way down, I understand."

"That's true all over the country, even in big cities," Maddy said.

"My hon became good friends with the former publisher," Ethel said, taking another swallow of her drink. "It began when Jer started circling mistakes in the newspaper—in red ink, for goodness sake—and mailing them to him. One day they met for breakfast and became fast friends. Even though Jer and I are liberals with a capital *L*, and the publisher was right of center. You see, my husband could get along with *any*body."

"You must miss him," Maddy said.

"Every day and every night," Ethel said simply. "So you are looking for a job?"

"Yes," Maddy said, glancing at the opened classified section.

"What kind of work do you do?"

"I worked for a small marketing firm, doing their graphic-design. But that was a few years ago," she said. "I am starting as a baker at Caboose Coffee this week, but that will not be my only job, or, how to say it, my 'real' job."

"That whole world of marketing seems interesting," Ethel said. "Convincing people to do or buy something."

"It is," Maddy said. "Especially when you're

designing something for a company or person you believe in. But when I got married, I let it all go. Looking back, I do not really understand why."

"For love?"

"Something like that," Maddy answered, remembering Arthur hounding her to give up her design work, so she could be a homemaker and support him in his goal of becoming a federal judge. Why had she caved? She saw a flash of red in one of the fruit trees.

"What's that bird?" she asked, happy to change the topic of conversation.

"A house finch, male," Ethel said. "Several species of bird visit us, though many will soon be gone now that it's getting colder. I have the finches and I especially love the cardinal pair that visits me in the winter, and my favorite is the arrival of the dozens of evening grosbeaks that come by every spring and sometimes the winter, on their way to somewhere else."

"You sound like a true birder," Maddy said, remembering how into birds her friend Belinda was. *Belinda.* There she was again.

"I have adored birds since I was a small girl," Ethel said. "I can identify most of them that come through, by sight and by their calls. And if I cannot, I pull out my *Peterson Field Guide to Birds of North America*. The illustrations are so beautiful. As a visual person, you would love them. I even have a few records of bird songs that used to be my mother's. I have never kept a life list or any of that nonsense. I just love them, feed them, and feel unaccountably happy when I see or hear them."

They finished their drinks in comfortable silence.

"Another?" Ethel asked.

"No thanks, but I so enjoyed this—the drinks and mostly the conversation."

"As did I, dear. As did I. And if you ever need to talk about something—anything—I am always here. And, by the way, I do *not gossip. Ever,*" Ethel said. "Good luck with your job hunt. Keep me posted."

They stood up, cleared the table, and walked into their separate homes, Daisy padding along behind her person. Both women thinking, *two straight lines, in rain or shine.*

Chapter 26

"I suppose you could say I needed a change of scene," Maddy said, hearing the cliché spill nervously out of her mouth.

She was sitting across the clutter-free desk from Detective Luis Ortega, the day after he had met her at the MoMo. She was trying to keep it simple, saying the truth, but not necessarily the whole truth.

"So you moved here from the Midwest?"

"Yes, from Wisconsin." How had he known that? She was sure she had not told Miles, plus she did not think Miles would have told Ortega, even if the two men were old friends.

"How did you find the Mountain Motel?"

"Online. It looked small and innocuous, but it had good reviews."

"What brought you out to Flagstaff in particular? Besides needing that 'change of scene'?"

Maddy felt her face flushing and cursed internally. She had always been bad at hiding her emotions, and knew that, as a detective, he must be good at reading people. She decided to be straight with him.

"Look, do I have to tell you the details of my life?" she asked. "I felt I had to get away, but I really do not want to share with you more than that."

Before he answered, she added more.

"If my name and location became public, it would

not be safe for me, I will just say that."

Ortega looked at her for what seemed like a full minute, and then nodded.

"Okay, Ms. Sullivan, I am going to take you at your word. I will contact you if I have any more questions." He took one of his business cards and jotted down his cell phone number on the back. "If anything comes to mind about your stay at the Mountain Motel, please call me. Even if it seems insignificant."

He waited for several seconds, as if giving Maddy time to come up with something, anything. Then he stood, and Maddy did the same.

"I appreciate your coming in."

"Did I really have a choice?" Maddy asked, feeling her old sense of humor surfacing.

He gazed at her and then smiled.

"Not really, but you would be surprised at all the people who are no-shows here."

"Maybe not so surprising," she said.

"Good point."

They walked to his office door, but Ortega paused before opening it.

"If you are in some kind of trouble with the law, I will find out. But if you have some other kind of trouble, feel free to talk to me. Come back, or call me. I mean any time. We may be able help you in more ways than you think."

Maddy was surprised by the tears that sprang into her eyes, and quickly blinked them away. *This seems to be a new habit. I am turning into an emotional waterworks.*

"Thank you, Detective Ortega," she said, glancing away from his steely gaze. "Best of luck with your investigation."

Through his office window Detective Ortega watched Madeline Sullivan walk out of the police-department building. He felt his frustration mount, though not related to this Flagstaff newcomer. She was obviously hiding something from her past, but he was certain she was no killer. His dark exasperation stemmed from the fact that an entire month had come and gone since the murder of Alejandra Lopez, with no suspect brought in yet. And now another killing. Ms. Sullivan has said "Good luck with your investigation." But now it was investigations—plural. It was his job to keep the community safe, and now to solve two murders. And he was failing badly. He needed to get a bead on the killer or killers, and bring them in. The whole town depended on that. Depended on him. Before the murderer struck again.

Chapter 27

The graveyard was quiet. It was a typical late October Flagstaff morning, and the monsoon season was finally over. Miles had arrived early on his bike and now stood at a fair distance from the open grave. He saw an unmarked police car drive up and park a half block away, and Luis Ortega stepped out of the car. The detective saw Miles and walked over to him. The two men shook hands, and then turned to watch as the mourners arrived.

"Here to show your respects?" Ortega asked his former roommate.

"I suppose," Miles said. "I guess I was just hoping there would be a good crowd to honor the boy. Plus, covering the murders, of course."

"Looks like more than family," Ortega noted, nodding his head toward the half dozen vehicles following the funeral home's black hearse.

"Yeah."

Miles saw Madeline step out of her new car.

"What is your take on Madeline Sullivan?" Ortega asked.

"Not sure. I've only had coffee with her and taken a hike—oh, and helped her move," he said. "Um, and had lunch with her. She was from somewhere back east, but I'm pretty sure she's got a Midwest accent."

Miles flushed, suddenly feeling like he was turning

into a spy for Ortega.

"Maybe not though," he added quickly.

"That's all? Sounds like quite a bit of contact to not even know where she is from," Ortega said, not letting on that he knew exactly where Madeline Sullivan was from. He watched the dead man's family and friends follow the funeral director over the grass to the grave. "And a newsman, besides."

"Yeah, I know. She doesn't seem to want to talk about her past. But, honestly, I have a feeling she may be trying to get away from it," Miles said, kicking himself mentally again. "Not sure though."

Ortega remained silent as he surveyed the crowd. Then he looked at Miles again.

"I do not want to be spotted with the evil press, so catch you later. My parents have been asking after you. How about getting a beer some time? So I can tell them you are still as bizarre a man as you were a teenage boy."

He walked away before Miles could come up with a decent retort.

Luis's parents, who now lived some fifty miles south of Flagstaff, had welcomed Miles for more than a few family meals. They had introduced him to real Mexican food, with hot red chile and pork tamales to die for. Luis's mom, especially, had taken a shine to Miles, while Luis's dad had teased the two young men about their potentially adversarial careers. When Miles returned to the Midwest to start his journalism career, he and Luis had talked every few months, catching up on former friends, their families, and careers.

By the time Miles had returned to Flagstaff for the newspaper job, Ortega had been promoted to detective.

Over the years they had shared information with one another, just to the point of it working for both of them. Well, mostly for Miles, he considered now. But maybe this time, he could help Ortega solve the mystery. *That would surely help get me off probation,* he suddenly thought. But he wasn't about to reveal any of these intentions to his former roommate. Better work on the murders as a journalist, and perhaps his digging would assist Ortega in the long run.

Before anyone else was murdered.

Miles could see the couple from the Mountain Motel—Karan and Urvi—and what he figured were their children—probably teenagers from the look of them. While the teens dressed in typical American clothing, Urvi was in a pale saffron-colored sari, and Karan was dressed all in white, a long tunic falling below his knees. The kids were between their parents, their arms around each other, and the parents and the girl were weeping. The boy looked stone-faced, no doubt shocked by his cousin's murder.

Another Indian woman, who must have been the dead boy's mother, was dressed in a white sari, and stood beside the grave, moaning. Urvi detached herself from her family and went to pull the other woman into her arms. They stood together, rocking and crying.

In addition to a couple of uniformed cops standing near their squad cars, Miles saw Charlie, her boss Ed Stenalp, and Beez, plus other members of the media like the guy Jared What's-His-Name who had originally replaced Charlie at the TV station and now wrote a local blog, but who, luckily for Miles, never seemed to scoop him as she had. His own boss Ruth was there, too, standing next to Lisha. He had told them he didn't think there would be many mourners, and it appeared they'd come out of respect. He knew the ceremony would have been different in India, where the body is often cremated.

And then Miles was surprised to see a couple of people who seemed way out of place.

Behind the gathering, standing on a small knoll, were two of the men who Miles had seen at the protest last—what?—last month was it already?

The ones who had spouted racism, as well as anti-immigrant sentiments. What the hell were *they* doing here? He watched Ortega clock them, too. The detective did not move toward them but remained in place as the funeral director said a few words. Miles was too far away from the group to hear what the man had to say.

He watched Madeline hug Karan and Urvi, say something to the two kids, and walk back to her car. Miles started to walk over to meet her, but saw Ortega wave to the uniformed officers and the three of them head toward the grassy knoll. Miles strolled over, keeping his distance. He knew if Ortega noticed him, he'd order Miles to stand back. Or, rather, to get lost.

So stand back he did, but was still able to see the two men speaking with Ortega. The tall guy Stan the van man was doing most of the talking, the shorter one nodding along. Harold, was it? Ortega turned to the street cops, said something, and Miles watched those cops start to take down the men's information as Ortega walked away.

Miles turned to see that Madeline's Subarubie was gone. She must have seen him, right? Well, it's not like they were at a typical social gathering.

Get a grip, man.

Ortega joined him, and they walked together back to the road. The young man's family remained at the grave.

"What the hell were those guys doing here?" Miles asked. "You know, they were both at the anti-SB 1070 protest—protesting the protest. Stan something and Harold something."

"I know. They said they had been walking along Milton Road and they saw the hearse and a 'car parade.' That's what the short one called it. And decided to take a walk into the cemetery to see what was going on."

"A bit far-fetched, dontcha think?" Miles asked as he and Luis stood near his unmarked car. Luis was solidly built, with a thin black mustache, his dark eyes constantly probing. "Could it be like those murder mysteries where the killer always shows up on the scene later on, pretending to be just another rubber-necker?"

"Look, Miles, I know you think you can help solve the murder. But please do not get carried away. That is our job, not yours."

"I'm not here for that. You know I'm covering the story."

"I do."

"I don't think I told you that I saw some pretty strange graffiti downtown the other day," Miles said. "Stop the invasion, whatever that means."

"Maybe territorial tagging. I will pass it on to our gang task force," Luis said. "So where did your girlfriend run off to? I suppose she did not think this was the time and place to be wooed by you."

"Shut it, man. I told you, she's not my girlfriend."

“That’s good to know. I will keep that in mind when I ask her what she was doing at the cemetery.”

“You already know, Luis,” Miles said as he pulled his bike helmet out of his sling bag and clipped it on. “She lived at the MoMo when she first moved to town. The Mountain Motel. That’s how she met the owners.”

“I know that,” Luis said, smiling before adding, “Thanks, Miles. I appreciate your help.”

Ortega opened his car door.

“Wait, Luis. You don’t think—”

“Of course not, Miles. I leave that to you.”

The detective closed the door and drove off. Miles gazed after him, and then walked to his bike. Ruth and Lisha were gone, the street cops were back in their black-and-white, and the angry anti-protest protesters were no longer in sight.

The grieving family remained huddled together, and Miles suddenly was transplanted back in time to the double funeral his own family had held for his father and older sister. He shivered. The loss never went away completely. How could it? He would call his mom tonight to check in.

Miles hopped on his bike and pedaled toward the newspaper.

Chapter 28

Miles didn't get very far before he caught sight of the two anti-immigrant guys, walking into a Benny's restaurant not far from the cemetery. On impulse, he stopped his bike, locked it, and followed them in. They were waiting to be seated, and Miles stood silently behind them, wondering if he'd made a mistake coming inside. But he was able to eavesdrop on the two men who looked over the menu as they waited for a hostess.

"It was another one killed and good riddance," said the tall man called Stan. "But if we'd said that to the cops, they would have thrown us in their ridiculous excuse for a jail before we could say George Washington's slaves."

Both men laughed.

"Still though, nobody wants them dead," the shorter guy Harold said. "More like we want to send them back to their own countries—wherever the hell that is."

The hostess came up to them and smiled.

"Table for three?" she asked. By the time the two men turned in confusion to look behind them, Miles was already out the door.

He clipped on his helmet and rode off, but not before seeing Stan peering at him through the restaurant door, then turning to follow the hostess.

Miles arrived at the newspaper, wondering if he

should have questioned them. But he knew if Ortega found out, he'd be furious. Still, he kicked himself for the lost opportunity. In fact, it could have been part of his story. He turned the bike around, knowing he had just enough time to question the men and get back to the paper to pound out his story by deadline.

Inside Benny's, he walked to their booth where they were drinking black coffees and in deep conversation. Miles wished he could be a fly on the wall. Instead, he stuck out his hand.

"I'm Miles Harper, a reporter at the *Gazette* newspaper. Mind if I ask you guys a couple of questions?"

They both stared up at him. Finally, Stan spoke.

"You talked to me last month at the protest, didn't you?"

"I did. Stan, is it?"

"Stan Trumpet."

They still just looked at him, making no movement indicating he could join them.

"And you are?" Miles asked the shorter man.

"Harold Boyle. Whatcha want with us?"

His voice was scratchy, as if he suffered from allergies of some kind.

"I'm writing a story about the young man who was killed at the motel. I saw you two at the cemetery and wondered if you wanted to tell me how you knew him."

Just then the waitress came over with two plates of eggs, bacon, and toast. Miles heard his stomach growl, but he knew he couldn't afford to take the time to eat.

"Can I get you coffee and a menu?" the waitress asked.

Miles looked at the men. "Can you give me five

minutes?"

They nodded.

"I'll take a coffee with milk, whole milk if you have it," he said.

He saw the men watching him, looks of something he couldn't quite read on both their faces. Criticism of coffee with milk? He pulled a chair from a nearby table up to their booth.

"Hey, I grew up in the Midwest. Back home, milk in the coffee is almost law."

No response as the two tucked into their meals.

"So how did you know Mr. Shukla?" he asked, pulling out his notebook and pen.

"Who?" asked Boyle.

"Hey, what's with that?" asked Stan, mouth full of toast, nodding at the notebook.

"Just to take some notes about the guys—who came to pay their respects and all."

"That was his name, Shukla?" Boyle asked.

"Rafat Shukla," Miles said.

"Hmm-mph," Boyle grunted. "It's not like we did anything illegal by showing up there. Those coppers were all over us."

"Yeah, they were," agreed Stan, sipping his coffee. "We told them we were just walking by and saw the funeral rig and cars and decided to see what was up."

"So you didn't know Rafat?"

Both men shook their heads, seemingly unconcerned.

"So we got nothing for you and your story," Stan said. "Sorry to hear some guy got killed, but we just ended up there, like, on a nice day. Know what I mean?"

Miles nodded and put his notebook away.

"One more question though," he said. "You guys were at the protest saying all kinds of things against immigrants. And then you happen to show up for a dead possible immigrant's funeral? Seems kind of too much of a coincidence, don't you think?"

The two men stared at him, their food forgotten.

Miles wondered, hoped, they were about to make a giant confession.

"You think if we killed that guy we'd go to his gravesite?" Stan asked. He laughed then, and Miles saw half chewed bacon caught in his teeth. "What do you take us for: idiots?"

Both men laughed then and turned back to their breakfasts, tuning him out.

"Time for you to scram, Miles Harper," Stan finally said. "And before you go accusing other random people, I recommend you be sure you got something real on them. Otherwise, you'd better be watching your back."

"A killer wouldn't stand for being accused by some fake news person," added Harold.

Miles pushed his chair back. He realized this was an idea that probably went to the top of his dumb-idea record. He sure wouldn't tell Luis about it. He practically accused these two guys of murder, simply on the basis that they were racists, or at the very least anti-immigrants.

He got back on his bike and rode again to the newspaper without any profound quotes or, better yet, a full confession from the killer, or killers.

Chapter 29

"In the past two years, the Arizona Legislature voted against bilingual classrooms. Our governor pretty much went along with them. And then the state passed this bill to get rid of any teachers who had thick accents," Miles told Maddy.

"Not really," Maddy said.

"I'm not making this stuff up, Madeline."

They were walking in Buffalo Park, the green space in the center of town that included a two-mile loop popular with runners, walkers, and their dogs. A weekday afternoon, the park was relatively quiet. Daisy kicked up dust on the trail ahead. Even in November the trail was dusty, given the decade-long Southwestern drought. The breeze grabbed it and carried it away. The air was much cooler than just a week earlier.

"And then there's SB 1070," Miles continued, his voice outraged.

"Senate bill?" Maddy asked, thinking her new friend could be a bit too passionate about this for a neutral journalist.

"Right. Senate Bill 1070 says cops can pull over anybody who looks like they might be here illegally. They call it the 'show me your papers' law."

"Meaning?"

"Meaning if I were walking down the street or driving my car—"

"If you had one," Maddy quipped.

"If I had one. Nobody would stop me. But if my skin was dark and, say, I tucked my jeans into my boots and greased back my hair, I'd be stopped because some officer, well, can. He makes assumptions. The law backs him up. Then, if the hunch is right, the guy can be deported on the spot. Nobody even has to inform his wife and kids who are at home during all this."

"Wow. There's tons of racism in the Midwest, but not like this—through legislation—that I know of."

"Racial profiling, plain and simple," Miles continued, barely taking a breath. "The bill is basically a grab bag of measures to enlist cops to expose and kick out undocumented workers. The Arizona legislators even want to reduce the teaching of ethnic studies and get rid of Spanish accents of teachers."

"You're not being a bit dramatic?"

"It may sound over the top, but you gotta read this bill, Maddy. It says that if you don't have immigration documents, it's a misdemeanor, sure, but one that can get you kicked out of this country on the spot."

"Wow."

"Puts a whole new spin on that charge-card ad, how does it go? 'Whatever do you have in your purse, or something like that? Don't leave your house without it.' "

"Uh-huh."

"Sorry. Didn't mean to give you a lecture."

They stopped walking and both looked up at the Peaks. The gold of the aspen was long gone. The chilly wind that whipped over the mesa announced that winter was just around the weather corner.

"So what happened to a reporter being objective?"

Maddy finally put into words her question. In college she had taken a couple of journalism classes along within her Visual Communication major. They began walking again, Daisy, nose down, leading the way.

"I'm not going to lie and say I'm objective on this issue," he answered. "But when I report on it, I do interview sources from all different sides. So the reader has balanced information. But, in reality, a reporter's objectivity isn't all that it's cracked up to be."

"Really?"

"I just mean sometimes you need to do more than just offer he-said, she-said reporting," he said.

They walked from the sunshine into the shade of gambel oaks and ponderosa pines, passing one of the exercise stations on the path.

"Ethel told me something I found strange," Maddy said, changing the subject. "She told me about her son, who sounds like a real piece of work. He's focused on moving her out of that house and into some kind of 'community' living."

"That is weird. She seems so great, at least on first impression."

"Families," Maddy said, shaking her head. She whistled for Daisy so the dog would not get too far ahead. Daisy came bounding back for a pet and took off again.

"Yeah, right. Got sibs?"

"One of each, but we're not that close anymore," she said.

"Your parents still alive?"

"Both gone. My dad died a long time ago, and my mom just three years ago. My grandmother helped raise us after Dad died. She's gone too, now. Oh, I had not thought about it until just now, but Ethel feels like family. Like I found a new grandmother."

"Very cool."

"What about you?" she asked.

"My dad and older sister were killed in a car crash when I was a teenager," he said, feeling the familiar gap suddenly pulsing inside him.

"I am so sorry, Miles."

"It was rough. Fran was my best bud. Now it's just me, my mom, and my kid sis. Type *A* achiever—or rather turned into one after they died, even as a little girl. She doesn't have a lot of time for family right now. So, my mom and me, we're pretty tight."

"Must have been so tough for her—for all of you," Maddy said. "But I am just thinking of raising two kids in the midst of her grief along with your sister's as well as yours."

"It sucked for everyone. But, yeah, she did one hell of a job."

They walked in silence for several minutes, headed up the hill.

"By the way, my close friends call me Maddy," she said, surprising herself.

"Hey, Maddy," Miles said, smiling but then turning serious. "About the murders."

"Yes?"

"They were both working graveyard."

"Kind of a weird coincidence," Maddy said.

"You know what they say—whoever 'they' is—there's no such thing as a coincidence."

They walked back toward the parking lot with the large buffalo statue at the park's main entrance.

"May I tell you something off the record, Miles?"

"About the murders? Please!"

"It must stay between you and me, and you can not say anything to your friend Luis. At least not yet."

"Okay."

"Well, it's just that Karan told me his son has been acting very strange lately. I did not tell the detective that, but with the second murder right there at the MoMo, I am not sure. I suppose I am worried it could be related."

"Why?"

"Well, when I first got to town and met the two kids, Tanak was so open and sweet. Now he seems, well, shutdown, uncommunicative. I mean, it's a big change. Noticeable."

Miles felt his fingers literally itching for his pen and notebook.

"And I've been getting really weird vibes from Charlie," Miles told her. "The stuff at the observatory—the murder and then the coke I told you about—just don't add up."

"Have you asked her about it?"

"She's, like, stonewalling me big time. There's something going on that I'm just not getting. Last time we met up, I swear she was high. At work."

"Are you saying you think that that could somehow be related to the killing at the observatory?"

"Don't think so—I mean, the two must have been done by the same person. And what would Charlie be doing at the MoMo?"

"Could it be some kind of drug ring?" Maddy thought aloud. "Could Charlie *and* Tanak somehow be involved?"

"I cannot see Charlie killing anybody. I mean, she

might be a recent user, but that's a far cry from shoving a knife between somebody's ribs."

"That's what I think about Tan, too. But, then again, I do not really know him."

"I used to know Charlie, but she seems like a different person these days."

They walked, both thinking of the ramifications of their conversation. Miles stopped in front of a tall green plant.

"You know this plant?"

"Why do I think I am about to find out?"

"Mullein. It's used by Native healers to help eliminate coughs, soften dry skin, and other stuff. The myth is that the taller it is in the fall, the harsher the winter will be."

They both looked at the plant with the soft leaves. It came nearly to Maddy's collar bone.

"This is tall, I take it?" Maddy asked.

"Taller than last year. And I hope that really means we'll have some decent snow this winter. I love cross-country skiing and snowshoeing! Good thing you got yourself that shiny new vehicle. It looks like you'll need it in Flag. Friends will be hitting you up for rides."

"Including you, I take it?"

"Ain't too proud to beg," *sweet darlin'* he thought but didn't say.

"*Baby, baby*. The Temptations. Face it, Miles, just like all journalists, you have a little knowledge about a lot of unrelated things," she said, surprising herself by laughing—for real—for the first time in, well, a long time. "Oh, hey, I forgot to tell you. I started as a baker at Caboose Coffee. On-the-job training, thank God. I have never been much of a cook or a baker."

"Good for you. That should be fun. I'll have to detect your baking in my next muffin."

They got to Maddy's car. She whistled for Daisy, who trotted over and jumped into the way-back of the winter-ready vehicle. As soon as she closed the hatch door, Miles's phone rang its Rock n Roll tune.

"The Byrds?" Maddy asked.

"I'm impressed," Miles said, struggling with his irritating phone holder.

"My dad was a fan. You're a bit young, though."

"I'm all things '60s," he said, then put the phone up to his mouth. "Yeah, Ruth?"

He ducked his head apologetically to Maddy and turned away from her.

"Uh-huh," Miles said, and then listened. "Right. I'll head over now."

He hung up.

"The cops are swarming a motel near campus. One of our ad people called it in. Speaking of begging for rides, can you give me a lift to my bike so I can get over there?"

They climbed into the car, slamming the doors shut.

"Sure. Or where is it? I can take you."

Miles said he'd direct her, and they took off onto Cedar Avenue, headed west.

Maddy could not help smiling. Apparently, she could look forward to a snowy winter.

"Nice wheels," Miles teased, perhaps reading her mind. "Love that new-car smell."

"One of these days, maybe you will get one."

"A new car?"

"A car, period. You should think about it. They're

the latest invention for up-and-coming reporters."

"At least I'm not increasing the carbon footprint," he said, as Maddy sped toward Route 66.

"Not that you seem much opposed to taking rides from people who *are* increasing it," Maddy pointed out.

Though given Miles's story of his father's and sister's deaths, Maddy reflected, *it made sense he did not want to own a car.*

"A guy's gotta do what a guy's gotta do."

Chapter 30

Maddy drove fast down the hill, turning west on Route 66 and then going under the railroad underpass onto Milton Road. The street was an odd mix of one-story older motels with peeling paint and worn-out roofs, and newer, chain hotels pushing their predecessors out. Those came between gas stations, restaurants, and small businesses, all trying to hang on. University buildings bloomed on the east side of the road, lots of red stone buildings just inside the university's north entrance. They arrived at the Motel 8.

"Don't pull into the motel lot. Stop over at the carwash next door, would you?"

Miles rifled through his backpack, pulling out his tools—reporter's notebook, digital recorder, and a couple of pens. "I'm counting three unmarked cars."

Maddy pulled into the carwash parking lot. "And two black-and-whites," she said, referring to the Flagstaff police cars. "I can stay here until you're done."

"Come along," Miles said without thinking. He opened the door before she was at a complete stop. "You could be a helpful observer. That is, if you want to." He turned toward the motel and started walking.

Maddy left the windows open a crack for Daisy, beeped the door locked, and jogged to catch up to Miles.

Detective Luis Ortega looked up from behind one of the two unmarked cars that formed a barrier between police and the motel. He shook his head impatiently when he saw Miles and Maddy but waved them over and down.

"What the hell, you idiot! Get down before you get yourself shot," Ortega greeted Miles. "Stay behind the vehicles."

He turned to Maddy. "You are here why, Ms. Sullivan?"

"I drove Miles here," she answered, realizing how silly she had been to do more than just drive him to the scene.

"Another one of his adopted drivers," Ortega said, glaring at Miles.

Miles realized his folly in asking Maddy to come with him. What was he trying to do, *impress her,* for God's sake? He felt his neck turning red.

"Stay down, both of you," Ortega said, turning his attention back to his officers.

"This related to the murders?" Miles whispered.

"Maybe. We just established a watch on the perimeter. We cleared the place. Most of the guests were already out. Two of my men are talking to the manager now. And that is definitely off the record. Or I will ask you to leave right now, Miles."

He waited until Miles acknowledged that with a nod.

"They're getting the keys to room 231. That is where the bastard's been living for about a month. We *think* he could be our guy."

"So from right about the time the Mars Hill murder happened," Miles whispered to Maddy.

"Thanks, Miles," Ortega said sarcastically, as if Miles was informing him. "Now shut it."

Two police officers were clearing the motel parking lot, one talking to a woman with a child who stood outside a room on the first floor. She grabbed the kid and went away from the motel and toward the carwash.

Maddy counted two snipers on the roof of the carwash and noted that a police car was blocking the entrance driveway there, too. She glanced back at her car but could not see Daisy. The dog was probably taking a nap after their walk. She was glad she'd parked away from the motel.

"Still off the record? We got an alert from the National Sex-Offender Registry folks. Routine notice about offenders not registered in the state," Ortega said in a low voice, chewing his gum with a vengeance. "This guy's name popped up. We tracked him to here. Manager said he's been staying here since the day before the first murder."

"A sex offender?"

"Yeah."

"But there wasn't anything sexual about the murders, was there?" Miles whispered.

"Not that the M.E. found, no," Ortega admitted, referring to the medical examiner, who examined the bodies and determined cause of death for the city and county. "But we're still hopeful because of the timing."

"Name?" Miles asked, hopefully.

"Cannot give you that yet."

Maddy was struck by the odd rapport between the two men. Not what she thought was common between journalists and the police.

Two officers, a broad-shouldered man and a petite woman, came out of the front office, guns at their sides as they walked up the outside staircase to the second floor of the two-story motel.

"Look," Maddy whispered. "That second-floor window, third from the left. The blinds just moved."

Ortega pulled out his radio. "Movement in the target area," he said. "Use extreme caution."

Maddy saw the female cop press her ear and nod. She must be wearing an ear bud to keep the radio from being overheard by others.

The three of them watched as two SWAT police dressed all in black came up behind the two officers at the door. The male officer knocked, and they could hear "POLICE!"

The door opened a crack, closed again, and just as it looked like the police might force it open, it opened wide. The man had apparently been loosening the door chain. Even from below, they could see him swaying on his feet. A white guy with close-cropped hair, he was wearing jeans and a T-shirt. They could see him talking to the police but were too far away to hear the conversation.

"Put up your hands," Ortega breathed out. "Or give us one damn reason to take you down."

The man did not do so. The officers grabbed him under his arms, handcuffed him to no resistance, and walked him, unsteady on his feet, down the stairs. It was over. The female officer escorted him to the police car, holding the top of his head as he awkwardly sat back into the seat. She said something to the cop behind the wheel, and then walked back up the stairs to join the other officers in the motel room. The car took off.

"Didn't have much to say for himself," Miles noted.

Luis Ortega clicked his radio.

"Clear his room. Roof shooters, stand down."

Maddy watched as the snipers dropped out of sight.

Ortega stood up and turned to Miles and Maddy.

"We will be interviewing the bastard at the station. I can probably give you a statement in a few hours," he said to Miles, then turning to Maddy.

"Good to see you again, Ms. Sullivan."

"Sorry I came along, Detective. I was not really thinking," Maddy said.

"That often happens when people are around one Miles Harper," he said, straight-faced. "Take note." He gazed at Maddy for a few seconds, and then walked toward the motel, gum popping.

Miles and Maddy walked back toward the carwash. A cluster of people watched from behind an improvised police barricade—a couple of sawhorses wrapped with yellow police tape.

"What's going on over there?" asked a teenaged girl. A tattooed tree grew up her arm, leaves fluttering on her neck and disappearing into her hairline.

"Busting somebody," Miles said. "No fireworks though."

"No fireworks," repeated a guy in a dark blue hoodie, as Miles and Maddy walked past. "No fireworks at all."

"Can we go back to our room now, Mommy?" a small boy asked. He was wearing pajamas with a puppy print that, despite the circumstances, made Maddy smile.

"Not yet, baby," his mom said, pulling him close.

"Soon."

Maddy unlocked the car, they buckled up, and she made what Miles considered a heroic left turn back onto Milton Road.

"Good driving skills," he noted lightly, then fell into an uncharacteristic silence.

"What?" Maddy finally asked.

"Well, how often do you have a sex offender who suddenly turns into a murderer? I mean, I don't understand why Luis was so hot on this guy being the murderer."

They were both quiet as Maddy navigated the car back toward the newspaper office where Miles's bike was parked. After taking a deep breath, she broke the silence.

"Look, Miles. I do not want to say much. But I have some experience with, uh, sexual deviants and the violence that can follow."

"Yeah?" Miles looked over and saw her face was lined with strain. "You okay?"

"Confidentially, and I mean that, the man I was married to, actually am still married to but I hope not for much longer was, well, had some serious sexual issues. I would rather not go into all that, but just to say that he went from a sex addict to something much more violent. His abuse was escalating. He has not killed anyone—that I know of—but I honestly would not put it past him."

Her last sentence surprised her, and she realized with a jolt how true it felt. She experienced the now-familiar creep of coldness streaming into her hands and feet, as if Arthur were hidden just outside her peripheral vision. She told herself to not look in the rear-view mirror for his black BMW. But then she did. The car was not there. Of course it was not, she chided herself.

"You must think I was crazy to marry him. But he was not like that at first. At least, I did not see that side of him initially."

"No. I get that," Miles said, though he didn't really.

She pulled over outside the newspaper office. A few late-falling orange leaves covered Miles's bike seat. Maddy was already feeling angry at herself for saying anything to Miles about her horrid marriage. He would probably judge her and not want to be friends. That was okay. She was fine on her own. Better than fine.

"Thanks for letting me tag along, and for the politics and nature field trip," she said, aiming for a light tone.

"Sure. Right," Miles said, adding carefully, "Hey, you doin' all right?"

"Fine," she said. She stared straight ahead, focusing on her breath, the way the counselor had taught her.

"Listen, you ever want to talk about that—about anything—I'm here for you, Maddy."

"Great. Thanks. Have a good rest of your day."

He squeezed her shoulder, but very gently she noticed, and then leaned into the back to give Daisy a pat.

"I mean it," he said, getting out of the car and turning back before shutting the door. "Any time."

"Bye, Miles," she said. She drove away without looking back.

Miles watched her car moving away, his heart cracking for her.

Back inside her house, she poured a bubbly water into a glass, gave Daisy a dog treat, and settled onto the couch. The dog jumped up beside her, instinctively putting her head on Maddy's lap, and gracefully accepting pets on her soft head.

Maddy's heart raced. She remembered the first time she and Arthur made love in that BMW. It seemed so romantic at the time. It was night-time in Lake Park, and he had parked overlooking the ravines leading to Lake Michigan. He had been so loving then, she had thought. So warm, yet manly.

But the next time they went on a date in the car, he actually "took" her. No foreplay, no words of love. That was after they were married, and suddenly it seemed he thought he was allowed to do anything to her that pleased him, without any expression of love, or even affection. And soon, when she no longer wanted the touch of this man who had mysteriously become cold as a Lake Michigan iceberg, he got rougher. She remembered when he pulled her head back by her hair, ignoring her cries of pain.

She closed her eyes and breathed, in and out, in and out. She could block this out. That was surely behind her. Was it not? She thought of calling Belinda, but once again she chickened out. She would call her tomorrow, for sure. *Right, Scarlett?* She fell into a deep sleep and dreamed of Arthur being shot by police as he came out of the hotel room on Milton Road. She woke up before she knew if he had lived or died. It was dark outside, dark in the house. Maddy turned a table lamp on low, taking in the bright and cozy room. As she pushed away the bad dreams, her real-life nightmare reasserted itself, as a scene from her marriage unfolded in her mind.

Chapter 31

"You were flirting with one of my own goddamned lawyers," Arthur said in that quiet but volatile voice Maddy had come to know—and fear. It was just past the two-year anniversary of their wedding, and she had not yet learned to keep quiet when he criticized her actions. For nearly a year, Arthur had been the doting husband, surprising her with expensive gifts for no special occasion except to show her "the extent of my devotion to you, my darling." The words had seemed thrilling at first, but soon sounded somehow empty, or right out of a movie script. That was because his initial charming devotion had turned into obsession. "What have I done wrong?" she continually found herself thinking.

"How could you embarrass me that way in front of my entire staff?" he demanded. It was the morning after his office Christmas party, where she had made a point of talking with as many people as possible, attempting to be the boss's good wife.

"What do you mean? I certainly was not flirting with anyone."

"Do not *lie* to me."

Maddy watched the muscles around his jaws tighten as they sat at the kitchen table. She took a sip of her grapefruit juice.

"I am not lying. I was trying to be a good partner to

you, to help put people at ease."

"Oh, like Daniel McGuire, my new lawyer? You practically threw yourself at him."

"I thought you wanted me to be more social," she said, recalling how the month before he had complained that she was not being a supportive wife. She could hardly keep up with his changing demands—and moods.

"I want a wife who respects me. And who keeps her hands off my people."

"Arthur, I am a friendly person. That is who I am. That is who you married. But I promise I was not—"

"Do *not* interrupt me."

Maddy was appalled, and then incensed.

"We are having a conversation, Arthur. Okay, maybe a fight," she said, taking a deep breath. "But there are two of us in this room. And I am *not* one of your underlings who you can boss around."

He stood up suddenly, stepped toward her, and yanked her up by her wrists. Daisy jumped up from her dog bed.

"And as far as Stella Hughes, stay away from her, too."

Now Maddy felt seriously confused.

"Wait, your new office receptionist? Did you think I was flirting with her too?" she said, laughing, trying to lighten the mood. Unsuccessfully.

"I would not put it past you, Maddy," he said, his eyes sparking. "That woman is trouble, and I forbid you from talking to her again."

"Arthur, I have no interest in socializing with anyone from your office," she said slowly. "But I do not take orders from anyone regarding who I can be friends with. And your resistance to my just being myself makes me wonder. What is going on?"

This slap came so quickly, she felt the sting practically before she saw his hand move toward her face. Daisy barked.

"Get your damn dog out of my house," Arthur said, a clear threat in his voice.

Maddy opened the back door to the yard and let Daisy out. The dog barked outside the door.

When she turned, she saw Arthur had grabbed his briefcase and suit jacket and was walking toward the front door.

"See you tonight," he said, as if nothing had happened.

"Arthur!" Maddy shouted, her palm on her warm cheek. Her answer was the front door slamming shut behind him. She heard his car start and drive away. She let Daisy back inside and sat down to massage her wrists. What the hell was happening?

Half a minute later, Arthur's phone beeped on the countertop. He never left it behind, so Maddy knew he must have actually also been upset when he left the house.

She swiped the phone open. Glancing toward the front door, she scrolled through messages on some dating app that he had left open. Dozens of conversations with women appeared, in which "ArtyBabe" told them exactly what he wanted to do to them. And details of in-person liaisons. Including one Ms. Hughes, his newest receptionist.

Maddy felt dizzy. She slammed down the phone and ran into the downstairs bathroom. She vomited up her breakfast staying on her knees for several minutes afterward. Daisy padded in, leaning into her.

How long had he been cheating on her? Why had he even asked her to marry him in the first place? And then it all made sense. All those out-of-town conferences he'd attended this past year, to which she had been firmly *not* invited. The local trial conferences that supposedly stretched into the night, when she'd known all along on some level that most courts call it quits around dinner time unless the jury is close to a verdict.

She heard the front door open and Arthur's footsteps on the thick carpet. She stood up, wiped her mouth, and walked into the front hall, phone in hand.

"Arthur," she said quietly.

"What now? I need to get to work."

"Arthur. We need to talk."

There must have been something in her voice because he turned toward her.

"I saw them."

"You saw what?" he asked impatiently, one hand on the doorknob.

"Your messages. Your affairs. Your other women."

Her legs began to shake, but she stood steady, hoping he would not notice.

"You looked at my phone!" he exclaimed. "I will not have you snooping in my private business."

"Private business? We're married, Arthur."

"I have a full docket today, Maddy. Get a grip on yourself. We will talk tonight."

"If you do not come home right after work, or if you decide you are not willing to talk this through, we are done, Arthur. I mean it. I am out of here."

Without answering, he took a step toward her,

seemed to think better of it, and turned to walk out the door.

That night, he came home at five o'clock with a bottle of champagne, a dozen dark pink roses, and Thai carry-out, her favorite.

"I adore you with my whole heart, Maddy. I do not know why I do not show my appreciation of you more," he started after laying out the meal at the long dining room table, putting their places right next to one another. "And with my job, sometimes I feel the pressure and I am afraid I have let that impact our relationship, our marriage."

"Your texts, Arthur. Your affairs."

"Those are fantasy. You did not think those were real, did you?" A tone of superiority was slipping into his voice. "Surely not."

"Arthur, I am not stupid."

Maddy pushed the pad thai around her plate, the way she remembered her brother used to when they were small and he was trying to hide his vegetables.

"Damn it all, Maddy. I will not be shamed for having found some release for my high-profile job, my stressful life."

"Some release from your stressful life," she said in a flat voice.

"Come on, Maddy. You know I love you. I would do anything to make you happy." He spread his arms out, looking around the room and beyond, to remind her of the beauty of the big house and lifestyle.

"But let us forget all that other stuff. And you know I can help you with that."

He got up and stood behind her chair, pulling it out slowly as he leaned down to kiss her neck.

"Hmmm, you smell good. I know what you want, Madeline Dempster."

"Arthur," she said so sharply that he stood up and moved away from her.

"I am not in the mood." It was typical that he refused to call her by her real name. He had never accepted that she had kept her maiden name. But that was not important now.

"Oh, come on. Remember the night, the month before we married, when we went to that bar in Scottsdale and role-played, and I was the knight, and you were my concubine? I tore your clothes off you—and we ravaged each other? I will be your willing slave tonight."

Maddy remembered the overpriced, overly air-conditioned hotel room with few features to set it apart from any others in the expensive Phoenix suburb. The requisite paintings of cacti and mountains in neutral shades graced the walls. She felt icy at the memory. Why had she gone along with whatever he wanted?

Now he knelt down, pulling hard at her clothes.

"Arthur, no!"

That's when he stood, slapped her again, picked her up, and carried her upstairs to the master bedroom, ignoring her protests as he took her. After, she went to the guestroom, locked the door, and pushed the dresser against it.

Never again, she thought. *Never*.

Chapter 32

Maddy sat up in her sun-soaked living room in her tiny house, stroking Daisy's head. She shuddered, remembering how, sometimes, she had even told herself how lucky she was that Arthur never slugged her with a closed fist. What a way to give him a pass, all the while denying her right to a healthy life, to happiness.

She recalled how, the day after he threw her onto their bed and raped her yet again, he had come home with a brand-new Mercedes.

"Gold, for my golden girl," he told her, that once-winning smile on his lips.

She had accepted it for the bribe it was. But it soon became the symbol of her hope, a financial escape tool. The cash for the car allowed her to leave with less stress about money.

She forced her mind back to the murder investigation now.

"Pretty pathetic when I would rather focus on murder than my past marriage, huh, girl?" she whispered to Daisy, the dog looking up from Maddy's lap.

Maddy wondered if the guy they had arrested was the killer. What a relief—for this town, her new home.

She recalled the way Detective Ortega had stared when they met that second time. Not like some guy ogling her. More like he was intrigued by her or wondering something.

"I hope I can share who I really am with people soon, Daisy."

Thump, thump, thump.

Chapter 33

Miles flopped into bed, then remembered his cell phone needed charging. He got up again and took it out of his holder. If nothing else these past few weeks, he'd at least learned to keep his work desk clean, well, cleaner, and his phone juiced up. He plugged it in, and it chirped once, and then beeped at him—two missed calls, both from Luis. *Damn it.*

Luis Ortega's voice was tired.

"Our man was so drunk we could not talk to him until late tonight. He finally said that he had traded his room with some guy. Probably our damn perp. He could not tell us anything about him. Oh, except that he was white—he thought. Could not say if he was tall or short, fat or skinny. Useless. We went back to doublecheck the Super 8 but of course the bastard was nowhere to be found. Looks like he wiped his room. Then he disappeared into the thin mountain air."

Ortega stopped, and Miles could hear the police-station noises of phones ringing and a distant siren.

"That is it, Miles. And pick up next time. As my father says, if you do not show up at the station, no way you are going to catch your train."

Miles heard Ortega's gum pop once before the line went dead. He hung up and smiled. He'd told Luis about screwing up at work, and how his cell phone had been resting under a mound of paper. His former roommate had only shaken his head in disbelief. Apparently, he had not caught the Instagram photo of Miles's desk. Miles had been in Ortega's office many times. Not a paper clip out of place, not one crooked photo, unlike most offices in the cop shop. Back when they were living together during college, their only conflict was over tidiness—or lack thereof. Ortega the neatnik; Miles the slob.

Miles looked back at his phone. Ortega had called an hour ago, and luckily for Miles it wasn't about another pending arrest or his ass would be fired by Ruth.

It hit him again. If he could figure out this case and get the Page One scoop, he'd be guaranteed his job. Wouldn't he? In the meantime, he was lucky he'd checked his phone.

"Fuckin' *fired,*" he mimicked aloud his boss's potty mouth. "You woulda been fuckin' *fried and fired Miles*."

He was grinning when his head hit the pillow.

Chapter 34

Miles walked into the police station, his mind buzzing as it struggled to fit together the pieces of the murder puzzle.

He stood outside Ortega's door, until his sometimes friend/sometimes source waved him in. Miles sat down across from Ortega as the detective finished a phone call.

"Catch you Saturday, if I can," Ortega said into the phone. "*Mi muy desaliñado* former roommate just showed. Thanks for your feedback, Pops."

He hung up the phone and looked at Miles.

"Your dad giving you some thoughts on the murders?" Miles asked, looking down at his only slightly wrinkled shirt. Who but Luis would consider it disheveled?

"You know how he likes to keep his finger on the pulse of things up here. And sometimes he really is helpful," Ortega said. "Then sometimes he just wants me to go fishing with him. He forgets the pressures of the job."

Ortega's father, Luis Sr., had been a street cop for nearly his entire career, never promoted higher than police sergeant. He and Luis Jr. were close, and Miles envied his friend's adult relationship with his dad, something he'd never have.

"Maybe he doesn't forget, but wants you to take a

break," Miles offered.

Ortega smiled. "Good point."

"So you said in your message, the guy was drunk, like sloppy drunk?"

"While I did not say sloppy drunk, I would not argue with that choice of phrase," Ortega said, watching Miles pull out his notebook and recorder. "We had to let him sleep it off before we could get anything out of him."

"And can I say for the record that you had a suspect but he was let go?"

"How about a 'person of interest.' He was never officially a suspect," Ortega said.

"You know, just because he was drunk, doesn't mean he couldn't have killed those two earlier," Miles pointed out.

"Why thanks for that tip, pal. Maybe you should apply to the police academy," Ortega said. "Seriously, though, we did look into his alibis for the nights of the murders. Turns out both of them were on a Tuesday night—"

"I hadn't realized that—"

"And he has a solid alibi for those dates. He was drunk watching and then sleeping at some kind of movie class held in the university library."

"Oh, the film class. It's a classic," Miles said. "Run by the Pauls?"

"Right, two professors with the first name of Paul. Both Pauls vouched for the guy. Said he was dead drunk—excuse the expression—on both our dates. They actually waited to escort him out of the building until after the last of their sensitive students left."

"I loved that class," Miles repeated.

"Sure could not have found many criminal-justice majors in that class when I was there. Talk about an easy A for you liberal artsy types."

Miles decided not to argue. He remembered it was one of his favorite classes—and while he'd received an A, it wasn't an easy ride to get there. The Pauls made students think.

"And is it fair to assume that the murders were done by the same person at this point?" Miles asked, bringing his head back to the present.

"Unless we have a very, very good copycat, yes, I would confirm that. Both victims were killed by multiple knife wounds. Both murdered in the hours before dawn," Ortega said.

"I wonder what the connection is," Miles mused aloud. "I mean, what did an observatory cleaner—someone who had only just come to see her relatives—have in common with a kid working at a motel on the other side of town?"

"I would not call the Mountain Motel exactly the other side of town," Ortega corrected. "But, still, I get your point. The two businesses do not have anything obvious in common. The observatory is world renowned. Its members are either local starry-sky nuts or international astronomers and other planet scientists. The motel is just an ordinary one that probably does not get a lot of celebrities staying there."

"Right. It's not the Monte Z or the Weatherton," Miles said, referring to two big-name downtown hotels that had been around since the early 1900s, even before Pluto was discovered. "And the drug connection?"

"We did not find any drugs on or around the body at the motel or up at the observatory. Still, with the cocaine Charlotte Thompson told us about, there could be something there. So we have not closed the book on that possibility."

"A bigoted murderer?" Miles said, mentally squirming in his seat, remembering how, over coffee at Benny's, he had practically accused the two anti-immigrant racists of murder.

"Could be, of course. But I do not really see that the crimes were driven by prejudice," Luis said, mulling it over.

"Unless it is prejudice about late-night workers," Miles joked.

"I believe there is too much anger behind the multiple stabbings of both bodies. Does not seem to be simply some racist who hates people of color," Luis said, ignoring Miles's joke. "I am not saying we have ruled that out though."

The two men sat in silence nearly a minute.

"My new beat officer talked to a couple of people who were standing across Route 66 from the motel after the killings," Ortega said. "Some older guy and a couple of joggers."

"He run their names?"

"Unfortunately, no. He's a rookie on our force. Though after I talked with him, I doubt he will ever make that mistake again."

Miles was pretty sure it was unlikely that anyone in Karan's family—even the teenaged son who Maddy had mentioned—had any connection to the observatory or to a drug circle. Plus, he'd promised Maddy he would not share her concerns about the young Tanak with Flag PD.

Also, Charlie had that whole thing going about her

employee needing drug rehab, and yet she was the one who had seemed high the other day, and who wasn't even doing her job well anymore—a first for her, as far as Miles could see.

Miles kept his thoughts about Karan Vohra's son to himself but brought Ortega back to Charlie and the cocaine found at the observatory.

"What about it?" Ortega asked.

"You know, do you think there's something there? I mean, where there's coke there's fire."

Ortega just shook his head. He was used to his old roomie's bad jokes.

"Okay, okay. But for real. If cocaine's on the grounds, maybe a deal went bad?"

"I cannot comment on the record about that, Miles," he said in a none-too-patient voice. "I will simply say we're looking at all angles and a variety of suspects."

"Okay, okay," Miles said, putting his pen down and pausing his audio recorder. "Can we just talk theories here? You know, put our heads together. Like the sheriff did with the locals in *Twin Peaks*."

As college roommates, the two had often focused on TV shows for purposes of making their arguments during their personal debates.

"Well, in that show, the FBI was in charge. But I get your point. Okay, so everything we say now is off the record unless you explicitly ask me if you can put it on the page. Got that?"

"I swear."

Ortega got up and closed his office door. "Turn that thing off. And not just on pause," he said as he walked back around his desk and sat down.

Miles did so.

"I have exactly ten minutes. What are you thinking?" Ortega asked.

"But first, off the record goes both ways, okay?"

"Up to a point, Miles. I will try not to burn you."

"Well, this may sound crazy, but it kinda feels like Charlie is in over her head on something. Like she's using drugs—I don't know that for sure, but the signs are there." He stopped when he noticed Ortega jotting down notes.

"Wait, she can't know any of this came from me, Luis."

"Calm down," Ortega said. "These are just for me. Not even my team will know where I got the information."

Neither of the men acknowledged that everyone in the force and beyond knew they were former roommates and sometimes friends. Somebody would figure it out, but not with any proof.

"Okay. And then there were the two guys at that SB 1070 protest—a handful of people who were protesting the protest, remember?"

Ortega nodded.

"Two of the guys who were there seemed really pissed off about immigrants taking all the good jobs. Then, and I know this is far-fetched," Miles continued, on a roll now. "But I get this strange sense about the guy Beez up at the observatory. He had some serious scratches on his face after the first killing."

"Beez?"

"He's a relatively new front-desk guy up there," Miles said. "Said he was attacked by his rose bush. He either felt awful about the cleaner getting killed, or he's a really good actor and was using that to play me. That's all I got, really. You?"

Ortega finished writing and looked up.

"I do not have anything more for you," Luis said, and Miles's eyebrows lifted. "Just yanking your chain, brother."

Miles smiled, relieved. "What can you tell me?"

"We are looking at a connection between the two places. There could be one based on drugs up at the observatory and the possibility that the young man at the Mountain Motel was dealing. Or that there is another dealer, fairly high up in the chain. Possibly he has been distributing at both places and thought he might be getting some competition. Again, that is completely off the record."

Miles nodded. Luis reviewed the notes on his laptop.

"And we have been tracking the movements of all of the anti-protesters from that day at the park rally. Nothing yet. I think that angle is a bit far-fetched. But that does not mean it may not be right on the money. We are looking at the two men who showed up at the cemetery. Plus that woman you interviewed—one of the anti-protest organizers––a J. Carruthers. Of the two men you interviewed, Harold Boyle apparently only arrived in Flagstaff by bus *after* the initial murder—he still had the ticket stub. And Trumpet we're keeping an eye on and certainly pulling him in to interview soon." Ortega looked over his notes again.

"I did not know anything about this man Beez, so I appreciate that. Know his real name?"

"Beasley. Irving or Irwin? I'll check my notebook."

"Do not bother. I will send someone up Mars Hill. What about the Mountain Motel owners and their kids? Anything?"

Miles felt his mouth go dry. He wanted to honor his agreement with Maddy, but also to find out what Ortega was thinking along those lines.

"You got something on him, er, them?" he asked.

Ortega looked up from his computer, his eyes laser-beaming into Miles's in that unnerving way they had.

"Him?" Ortega asked with obvious interest.

"Him, them, her, I don't know, Luis," Miles said quickly. "Do you have any suspicions about the family? I think there are the parents and two teens, yes?"

"And the aunt, a single mom, whose son was killed," Ortega said, finally turning away from Miles's face and back to his notes.

"Right. Think any of them could be involved?"

"I do not want to go there at the moment, Miles."

That door firmly shut, Miles started to pack up his things, and then stopped. He turned on his recorder again.

"So your formal statement for my next update in the paper?"

"Flagstaff police are pursuing several leads on the two murders," Ortega said. "We cannot say if they are related. No, scratch that. We have not yet *determined* if they are linked. We understand the community feels unsettled. We are working hard to solve these killings. To bring the killer or killers into custody."

Miles packed up his notebook and recorder, got up, and reached over the desk to shake hands.

"Thanks, Luis."

"Listen, there's one more thing, Miles."

Miles, surprised, sat down. Usually after a formal statement, that was it. Luis's ten minutes had come and gone.

"Yeah?"

"This is a bit sensitive, but how well do you know the woman Madeline Sullivan? The one you were trying to impress at the Route 66 motel? Which, by the way, was completely unprofessional. To arrive unannounced, sure, but to bring somebody along for show and tell. What was with that?"

Mils felt his face burning. He couldn't deny it.

"Bad idea, I agree," he said. "I was just being stupid. Really, really stupid. What about her?"

"I am asking the questions here. Again, how well do you know her?"

"Not all that well. She moved here a month or two ago. We met at Caboose Coffee."

"And?"

"And what?"

"Let me be blunt. Are you seeing her? As in, sleeping with her?"

"Jesus, Luis! I'm not telling you that!"

"Okay, so you are not," Ortega said with a glimmer of a smile, then turning serious again. "But I mean it, Miles. How well do you know her?"

"Not all that well. I like her a bunch, as you've guessed, but she's not that easy to get to know, honestly. She hasn't talked much about herself."

As he spoke, Miles realized how elusive Madeline/Maddy had been about herself, her life.

"She's got a cool dog?"

"Listen, bud, her name popped up out of Wisconsin

on the national missing person's system. But when I looked at the details and checked her background, it made me pause. I did not alert the system about her yet. And I interviewed her without saying anything about this. But I wanted to know if you knew of anything."

"I'm not your spy, Luis."

"For God's sake, Miles. I was just asking in case she had said anything that would indicate she was in danger. And for double God's sake, this is more than off the record. Do *not* let her know I mentioned her. Got that?"

"Sure, sure," Miles said, and meant it.

As he was walking out of the cop shop, though, he felt concern washing through his entire body. He could swear his heart was beating double time.

Was Maddy in danger? Was that why she kept so much to herself? What was going on with her? He remembered the pale band of skin on her left hand where a wedding ring would live. Was there anything he could do to help her? How could he find out, without letting her know what Ortega had told him? And why did he care so much about it, about her?

As he'd truthfully told Luis Ortega, he barely knew her.

Chapter 35

Maddy turned to the last of the boxes of books. The one that she had asked Miles not to touch. The one filled with books on domestic violence and codependency and narcissists and about how to flee a violent relationship. All self-help books, with a specific theme. She remembered the shame she had felt at the thought of Miles seeing the titles. But she should feel proud she informed herself and got out, not shame faced.

She vowed that now she would read more novels and fewer self-help titles. Still, she would not toss them out. She dusted off the wooden jewelry box that her Grandmother Alice had brought her from Cuernavaca when Maddy must have been about six. She remembered how excited she was, because a jewelry box seemed like something for a big girl. When she had opened it and found the bracelet of turquoise, she'd flung her arms around her grandmother, the woman who had helped raise the children after their father died. Grandma Alice, a reserved woman, seemed startled, even shocked at this display of affection. But she had hugged the girl back, and when they pulled away from each other, Maddy saw tears in her grandmother's eyes.

Maddy had long since outgrown the child's bracelet but still kept it in the box, along with other jewelry she'd accumulated over the years. Though not the diamond engagement ring or gold band from Arthur, nor the expensive pieces he had bought for her while they were courting. And then the ones that came as payoffs for his later violence. Those she had happily left behind. She centered the sweet box on the top of her dresser, willing herself to let go of thoughts of him, of their marriage, and of the time she now felt she had wasted.

She pulled up her sleeves. No more bruises. She was freeeeee.

Outside, she picked up the *Gazette* from the driveway. It was so thin, it looked more like one of those free advertisement throwaways. Still, while she was working at the Caboose Coffee bakery, she would peruse it every day in case a local company liked the paper more than Craigslist.

As she poured herself a bubbly water and glanced through the minuscule list of job offerings, she felt her heart's beat slowing down, along with a slight feeling of hope growing. She had not wasted those years. No. She had learned about herself and about manipulative people whose main attraction was charm. She was no longer the innocent small-town Midwestern girl. She would move forward from here, more savvy, less trusting, perhaps, but stronger and clear-eyed. Oh, and how about happy.

She was going to be fine. More than fine.

Thump, thump, thump.

Chapter 36

After ditching school early, Tanak walked around and around the duck pond, just a few blocks from the high school. It was dusk now, and he had been out for hours. Ducks floated serenely on the water, and the resident heron dove from its perch to pull a fish from the pond. It was peaceful. Maybe not for the fish, though.

He needed peaceful. He had to think. He could not get the smell of his cousin's blood out of his nostrils. Like salt and wet metal. That terrible day. What had he done to his cousin, who had only been kind to him, if a little distant? Rafat did not deserve such a violent, early death. Would Tanak's life ever be the same?

And then there was his concern about his little sister. It seemed the only way to keep her safe was more revenge. His parents, who always preached peace and love, would never understand.

Fists clenched, the teenager walked and walked, and walked some more.

Chapter 37

In Santa Fe, New Mexico, some four hundred miles east of Flagstaff, Arizona, a cell phone rang.

Belinda Rodriguez stood outside her adobe house, just home from work. She looked at her phone and saw that it was a Wisconsin area code. Was Maddy calling, finally?

"Hello," she answered, hope lifting her voice by an octave. "Maddy?"

"Nice try. Let me talk to my wife," a voice growled.

"Arthur?" Belinda said, stunned. She was shocked to hear the voice of her old friend's awful husband. She walked inside, and the soothing smell of red chile enveloped her. She barely noticed.

"Arthur, why are you calling me?" Belinda asked, setting her briefcase on the front-hall table and kicking off her low pumps.

"Do not play dumb. I have the right to talk with my wife. Is she there with you in California?"

"What's happened? Is Maddy okay?" Belinda asked, not correcting him on her location.

"I *said* do not play dumb with me," he repeated, his voice more animal than human. "I know you have been egging her on to leave me ever since she and I met. She's probably standing right next to you."

Belinda took a breath.

"Arthur, she is not here. I have not talked with my friend for two years. You cut her off from me and the rest of the world. Tell me what happened. I'm worried that—"

"A married couple's business is private."

But then he wondered where his wife could be if this witch was telling the truth. He had to think. He *had* to find his wife and bring her home where she belonged—with him. *To him.*

"Where might she have gone?" he asked more to himself than to this bitch on the end of the phone call.

Belinda rushed in before he could hang up.

"Did you have a fight? Is she depressed? What?"

"We had an argument, but I was ready to forgive her. Then she vanished," he admitted, thinking perhaps she could come up with some idea where Maddy had ended up, if in fact the two were not together.

"Any ideas?" he asked, suppressing his contempt for her as long as needed. It was a courtroom trick that had stood him well over the years before he became a judge. Get their trust, get them talking, and then—bam!—once you get what you came for, shock them with the fact that the warmth was all pretense. His lips curled up at the memories of what he had come to consider "legal deceit."

"Does she still run? She could be lying on a trail somewhere. Or maybe she took off to, to think things over," Belinda said, making sure she didn't push him too far. "I know she's always been drawn to the West. Maybe some place she could get back to her career?"

Belinda stopped herself. *Wait! Why should I help this asshole find Maddy*?

"And I'm not trying to get into your business. I just

want to help my friend."

"As if. You have always been a jealous bitch," Arthur sputtered, done with the nice-guy act. "Jealous of Maddy's love for *me*."

"Arthur," Belinda said slowly now in her own cold voice. "If you ever contact me again, I will file harassment charges against you so fast your whole damn body will spin. And the State Bar of Wisconsin will surely think twice about any more support when it comes to additional public offices you may seek."

She recalled Maddy telling her a few years ago that Arthur had dreams of the governor's mansion. *More like dreams of power, any kind of power*, Belinda had thought at the time.

They both slammed their phones down, staring at them for a minute, and then turning away.

Arthur Dempster moved to his computer, searching for a distraction. He had an entire list of lovelies longing to hear from him. The situation with Maddy could wait.

Belinda, shaking with rage, walked into the warmth of the kitchen, where her wife Rosie had chips, guacamole, and two glasses of red wine waiting. A pot bubbled on the stove. They sat together in comfortable silence for several minutes, watching the sunlight fade on the Sangre de Cristo Mountains. The two had legally married in California two years ago. Rosie squeezed Belinda's hand but stayed silent.

Where could she be? Was she okay? Belinda wondered, returning Rosie's affectionate squeeze. She was struck that her best friend did not even know Belinda was married.

Call me, Maddy, she silently sent her hopes into the

New Mexico night. *Please call me, and let me know you're okay. I'm here.*

Chapter 38

Maddy woke with a start to the sound of a deep growl. She had been dreaming about being on a road trip with Belinda—as teenagers—along with a puppy version of Daisy in a multicolored 1970s VW bus. Maddy was behind the wheel. They were on a mountain road, racing downhill, both girls and even the dog laughing hysterically. But then Belinda's door flew open, Maddy could not find the brakes, and her friend's body was halfway onto the road when Maddy awoke. The skidding sound of the tires turned into real-life growls. Daisy growls.

She sat up, her night gown damp with sweat.

Daisy was standing at the front door, hair on her back raised, alternating between growling and barking.

"Come on, girl. I am not letting you get skunked again," Maddy said.

Several nights ago, Daisy had been whining to go out, and after Maddy complied, a skunk had sprayed the dog. After several doses of a mixture of hydrogen peroxide, dish soap, and baking soda, Daisy had nearly lost her skunky odor. Nearly. Maddy flashed on the old cartoons starring the French skunk.

"Ooh la la, Daisy! No way," Maddy said, rolling over, her back to her bedroom door. The glimmer through her curtains told her the streetlights were still on. She had worked at the bakery until one a.m., come home, and fallen into the sleep of the untroubled dead. Daisy whined again and licked Maddy's hand that hung over the side of the bed.

Suddenly, the dog was back at the door, barking furiously. Not a skunk bark. Maddy flashed on to the recent murders, her heart slamming in her chest. She grabbed her phone and was looking around for some kind of weapon, when she heard a soft knocking. She got up and went to the living room. Could her landlady need her for something at this time of night?

"Ethel?"

"Sweetness, it's me," came the sickeningly familiar voice that sent chills down her spine. "Open up, Love. Let me in. Come back to where you belong. With me."

Maddy felt nausea hit the pit of her stomach, her weak legs barely holding her upright. How had Arthur found her?

Should she stay quiet and hope he would think she was out? But she had already said Ethel's name. Should she call the police who might do nothing, given that he was her husband? Should she open her door and have a frank conversation with Arthur? She stared at her phone, paralyzed. Then, as Daisy charged at the door again, Maddy spoke.

"Go away, Arthur," she said, her voice quavering despite her best intentions of sounding strong. "It is over."

"Not for me. Never, my darling."

She raced back to her bedroom, as Daisy continued barking at the front door.

It made no sense, but instead of dialing 9-1-1, she called Ethel.

"Yes?" answered her octogenarian neighbor,

sounding sharp as a pin, despite the time.

Arthur's knocking turned into pounding.

"Ethel, it's my husband."

"Did you have a bad dream?" Ethel asked sympathetically.

"He's here. At my door. He's trying to get in."

"I am notifying the police, child. Do *not* let him in that house!"

As if.

Maddy dropped the phone when she heard Arthur's voice just outside her bedroom window. Thank God the temperatures had dropped, and just this week she had stopped sleeping with the windows open anymore.

"You're not very well locked up, darling," he said, his voice mocking through the thin layer of glass.

Daisy jumped up on the bed, charging the window, barking loudly.

Daisy had never liked this man, Maddy realized. *Smart dog.*

"Arthur, the police are on their way," she said, grabbing an unopened glass bottle of apple juice for a weapon. "You need to go. You need to leave me alone."

He laughed, and now his voice sounded on the edge of hysteria.

"And what will the police do to a man who is simply visiting the woman he loves, his *wife*? I do not believe law enforcement or the courts—even in this backwards Southwestern town—would have much of a problem with that."

Maddy heard sirens, and then the slamming of car doors.

"Next time, I will not knock, sweetness," Arthur

said, his voice fading as he moved away. "*My* sweetness."

Now came the sound of footsteps. Still, she held the bottle over her head, unable to put it down.

Daisy had finally stopped barking, but her head was turned at an angle, looking at the window from which Arthur had last spoken. She jumped down and trotted beside Maddy into the living room.

"Open up, ma'am. It's the police," came a low voice, as Daisy started barking again. Maddy grabbed her collar, though she seemed unable to move her feet.

"It's all right, Madeline," Ethel said. "You can come out now. The police are here. I am here."

Maddy opened the door, holding the dog's collar in one hand, and the juice bottle in another.

"May I come in, dear?"

Ethel followed a young officer in, looked around, and gently took the bottle from Maddy's hands. She opened her arms, and Maddy fell into them, her whole body shaking, tears cascading.

"Everything's okay now," Ethel cooed, gently walking them back outside.

A scattered bouquet of two dozen red roses lay on the ground outside her door. In the dark, the petals looked like blood.

"Sorry to wake you. I know I should have dialed 9-1-1. I was not thinking straight."

"How could you be?" Ethel said. "I would have awoken anyway with the police outside."

After doing a sweep of the small space, the first officer joined another one outside, and they stood in the yard behind Ethel. Daisy seemed to know not to bark at them. She sat at high alert beside Maddy.

"You had a prowler, ma'am?" asked the older and shorter of the two men. His muscles bulged through his uniform shirt. The younger one had the physique of a beanpole.

"My ex-husband," Maddy said, willing the "ex" part to be true soon. Now, there was no need to put off filing for divorce because he might find her.

She found it was hard to speak.

"She moved here from the Midwest this fall," Ethel took over. "She is on the run from a violent husband."

"I do not know how he found me," Maddy said in a small voice.

"Stop right there," shouted the younger cop. He shined his flashlight at a man running into the yard from Ethel's side.

Miles blinked in the light, which reflected off his glasses and bike helmet.

"Maddy, Ethel, everything all right?"

"This your husband?" asked the young cop, poised for a tackle.

"Hardly," said the older cop, guffawing at his new colleague. "This is the press. What are you doing up at this hour, Harper?"

"Heard it on the scanner and recognized the address," Miles said, his eyes switching back and forth between Maddy and Ethel.

A car door slammed and an engine started, and they heard a car peeling away. The young policeman bolted out to the street but came back walking.

"Large sedan, dark, some kind of Ford. Arizona plates but couldn't grab the number."

"Call it in," the older office ordered.

"Arizona plates?" Maddy asked, confused.

“Where does he live?” the burly officer asked.

“Wisconsin. Milwaukee. That’s where I moved from.”

“Probably a rental, miss,” he told her, his voice gentle. “If he flew here, makes sense he’d rent a vehicle.”

He turned to Miles.

“I hope you’re not planning on splashing this all over the front page. She is considered a victim, and it would not help them to have the publicity, no matter what your editors tell you.”

“No worries. They’re my friends,” Miles said. “I’m here as a person, not a journalist.”

“I couldn’t have put it any better,” the cop said dryly.

Miles ignored the joke, though later he admitted it was a pretty good one.

“When I heard the call go out with this address, I wanted to make sure nothing had happened to you two,” Miles said to the two women, who stood arm in arm.

“Why thank you, dear,” Ethel said, and linked her free arm through his. “It is good to have friends.”

“You have somewhere you can stay so you’re not here on your own, ma’am?” the officer asked.

“I doubt he would come back any time soon,” Maddy said, but even she heard the uncertainty in her voice. “Would he?”

“She will spend the night next door with me,” Ethel declared. “I have an extra bedroom and will turn on the alarm system.”

“I’ll stay, too,” Miles announced. He looked at Ethel. “Got a couch I can crash on?”

"I do. That would be grand," Ethel said. "All right with you, Madeline?"

"I will be fine," she said, but was contradicted by the officer.

"I highly recommend that you accept your friends' offer. Or we can get you settled in a motel room. I would not want my wife or daughter sleeping in that house after an incident like this," he said. Then, as if remembering a gender-equality workshop, he hastily added, "Nor would I want my son to stay here by himself after that happened, if I had a son."

Maddy looked at her friends. They were her friends, were they not? Exactly what she had hoped for upon her arrival to Flagstaff just—what was it, less than two months ago? Both Ethel and Miles were watching her, unable to disguise their concern. She saw the irony: It had taken Arthur's visit to help her realize she had real friends here.

"Sure. Let's have a slumber party," she said, not wanting to give in to Arthur one more time by leaving her house but hearing again the grim insistence in his voice. She would do this for herself, and for her friends, and not for him. She would not be a victim, but she would not be an idiot, either.

She gave the police a description of Arthur and agreed to come into the police station the next day—or, actually, later that same day given that it was nearly three a.m.

Ethel led the way into her house, with Maddy behind her, and Miles and Daisy bringing up the rear.

"Do you need anything from your place?" Miles asked. "Happy to go over and get something."

"No. Maybe in the morning."

Ethel nodded to the chairs around the kitchen table and got busy with ice, glasses, and a bottle of bourbon. “I do not normally drink in the wee hours, but I would call this an appropriate exception to any rule.”

She poured them each a couple of fingers into crystal glasses, and then put the bottle on the table, along with a small pitcher of water, in which nobody appeared interested. She raised her glass.

“To friends,” Ethel said.

“Hear, hear,” Maddy said, her throat nearly too full to swallow—but not quite. The whiskey burned her throat going down—in a good way.

“That is some good spirits,” Miles said. “Smooth.” But while his voice sounded bright, his worried glances at Maddy made it clear he was not feeling light-hearted.

It was Ethel who patted his hand.

“It is okay, Miles. Madeline is going to be fine,” she said, and then turned to her tenant and friend, patting her hand. “We’re going to help her get there. You deserve better, Madeline.”

“His voice was so scary,” she said softly. “It reminded me why I became afraid of him.”

She paused and then smiled briefly.

“Not sure what I planned to do with the bottle of apple juice,” she said.

“Apple juice as weapon?” Miles asked, though unable to smile.

“You were prepared to protect yourself by any means, child,” Ethel said.

The three talked about nothing else heavy, finished their drinks, and went to their beds—or couch.

Ethel fell asleep within minutes, Maddy was awake for an hour before falling into a fitful slumber, and

Miles tried unsuccessfully to stay awake.

It was still dark out when he awoke to a wetness on his elbow. Daisy was there, her wide nose pressed up against his arm, willing him awake.

“It’s all right, girl. We’re gonna keep her safe. You and me, Daisy,” he said, stroking the dog’s soft head. “Not to mention our super grandma.”

Miles glanced at the clock, which read five fifteen. The house was quiet, and he had no sense there was any danger. He was right, though only for the time being.

Daisy trotted out and back into the guest room, and Miles heard the squeak of bed springs. He could have sworn she was checking in, keeping Miles alert in case that horrible man returned. Horrible husband.

There were dogs, and there were dogs. And then, there was Daisy.

Chapter 39

Before slipping out of bed the next morning, Maddy dialed Belinda's number. It was past time.

"It's me," she said, her voice cracking at the sound of her friend's recorded voice. She felt gratitude that her friend had the same phone number. "This is my new cell. Um, um…" She searched for a way to explain, to tell her oldest friend about what had happened. But she knew some words could not be said over a phone message. "I am so sorry. I am sorry about everything, B. It's me, Maddy. Please call me back."

She hung up, happy to have finally made the call, and amused at herself. "It's me, Maddy," she repeated to Daisy, who lay beside her on Ethel's guest bed, chin resting on Maddy's chest. "As if she would not know." *How long has it been? Two long years? Nearly three?*

Maddy was smiling when she appeared in the kitchen to find Ethel sipping coffee and reading the newspaper. Three coffee cups were on the table, as well as a plate of what looked like blueberry scones. Ethel's smile matched hers.

"I am afraid you missed our white knight," Ethel said, nodding at the used cup. "He had to get to work. But he told me to tell you hello and said he would be checking up on you—on us—later today. Coffee?"

"Please." Maddy opened Ethel's kitchen door and let Daisy outside. She glanced toward the casita and felt an icy finger of fear.

"Obviously, you can stay with me here as long as you like, Madeline," said Ethel, apparently a mind reader. She stood up and draped a shawl over Maddy's shoulders. "I would love the company for as long as it suits you. But no obligation, of course.

"Thank you, Ethel."

Maddy took the coffee and helped herself to a scone.

"So how are you feeling this morning?" Ethel asked gently. "Did you ever get to sleep?"

The older woman knew she had, because she had checked on her that morning, as had Miles. The young man had been like a mama bear.

"I did, thanks. Fitfully, but still got some sleep. It's funny. I was having a nightmare just when he arrived at my door. But I cannot remember if I dreamed anything after I got here to your house."

The two sipped their drinks in friendly silence.

"Thanks again for last night," Maddy said. "For everything, Ethel."

"Of course, Madeline. That's what neighbors—and friends—do. Anyway, if you feel you need to get away for a bit, do not feel obligated to stay next door. I do not mind an empty casita for a couple, few weeks. And if there is an issue with the rent, I can keep it open for you for a couple of months. I like having you here."

Maddy felt moved again by this new friend, this gesture of kindness.

"I am fine for money, Ethel. Since you know so much already, I may as well tell you. He was feeling so damn guilty about smacking me around that he came home with a new Mercedes Benz CLS afterward. It's amazing how much you can make on a barely-used luxury car like that," she said, grinning.

Ethel giggled like a girl, and soon they were both laughing hard.

"You are a smart woman, Madeline."

"Thanks. I also had squirreled away some money that I never told him about. That idea came from my friend Belinda, who from Day One never trusted the guy. I still cannot believe I chose Arthur over her, my lifelong friend."

"Do not be too hard on yourself," Ethel said. "As I told you the other day, when it comes to matters of the heart, and under the influence of manipulative people—often narcissists—it is hard to understand our choices. But now you're in a great place. And I do not just mean in my kitchen!"

"Yummy scones," Maddy said.

"Jer's father brought this recipe home from the first world war," she said. "Always told us there was nothing like a scone made in England. His mother made them regularly and gave the recipe to me—I suppose to keep her son happy. Which it seemed to, come to think of it. We had them most Sunday mornings."

"Most scones I get are incredibly dry. Even at Caboose Coffee. These are so moist."

"One day, I will pass the recipe on to you," Ethel promised. "So what are your plans for today? Do you work at the bakery?"

"No, not until tomorrow night. I am so glad because I need to catch up on my sleep."

Maddy's phone rang, and she looked down. A New Mexico number.

"Sorry, Ethel. Do you mind? I do not know who

this is but I am hoping to hear back from Belinda. This could be her."

"Go ahead. And feel free to sit in my backyard if that's more comfortable for you at the moment."

Maddy stepped out back, wrapping herself in her landlady's shawl, and sat at Ethel's patio table. She took a big breath.

"Hello?"

"Maddy, Maddy, Maddy!"

Tears filled Maddy's eyes. It was her.

"Are you okay? I've been so worried about you," Belinda said. "Tell me you're okay before you say another word!"

Maddy felt confused. Did Belinda know Arthur had found her? She told her what had happened, that she was okay, and then they were both crying before they could say anything else. Once the tears stopped, Maddy apologized again for deserting her friend for nearly two years. She told her that once they could sit together in person, she would tell Belinda everything.

"Where are you?" Belinda asked.

"Flagstaff."

"Wait, what? I live in Santa Fe now. That's, like, five or six hours away from you. Okay, you're coming over here!"

Maddy laughed, remembering Belinda's bossy mannerisms.

"Or we could come to you. You know the train stops at both places, don't you? Well, just outside of Santa Fe."

Maddy was thrilled.

"I thought you were still in northern California," she said, relief flooding through her to finally be talking to her old friend again.

"Moved to Santa Fe about a year ago, but my old phone number forwards my calls."

"And who is 'we'?"

"Haha, you'll have to find out when you come," Belinda answered. "But I love her. It's real—and, even better, it's mutual!"

Maddy could practically hear her friend's smile through the cell phone towers' electromagnetic radio waves. Then Belinda's voice turned urgent.

"You should come here sooner than later, Mad, considering that late-night visit. He sounds unhinged. We can put you up. There are tons of good design jobs here for someone with your talents. Please say yes?"

"Give me a couple of weeks, will you? I just started working at a late-night bakery—"

"A bakery? What are you thinking?"

Maddy was not offended by Belinda's question. If nothing else, her friend had always been blunt—to the point where some people thought her too much. She was the only person with the courage to warn her about the potential shadiness of Arthur's character. Had she only listened.

"Honestly, B, I did not want to take any job that might help Arthur find me. You know, like anything at a marketing firm or graphic design studio site that would require a social-media or online presence. Do you get that?"

"I do. Listen, I'm afraid I may have helped that bastard find you," Belinda said, her voice suddenly low. "I've been beating myself up about it, and now that you told me he found you, well. I hope it wasn't because of me."

She told Maddy about the strange call she had received from Arthur just a week earlier, and how he'd been obsessed with tracking Maddy down.

"And then, well, Mad, I ended up saying something about how you always wanted to live out west or were drawn to the Southwest. I just hope he didn't put two and two together."

Maddy wanted to soothe her friend.

"Do not worry about it. I mean, now that it is clear where I am, and the police have him on file, I am actually relieved," she said. "Anyway, reminding him what I must have told him more than a dozen times but he clearly was not listening—that I loved the idea of moving out west—does not mean you really revealed anything. Actually, it shows how self-centered he is that he never listened. I still do not know how he found me."

"You sound good, Maddykins, all things considered," Belinda said, reverting to her friend's childhood nickname. "Listen, I gotta get going. Talk to that damn bakery and find a time you can get just a couple of days off and come over. If not, I'll come to you next month, okay?"

"I will. And thanks for forgiving me, B."

"Don't be crazy, girlfriend. We've always been there for each other—and forgiveness is just part of friendship, right?"

"You are so right. Talk to you soon. Love you."

"Love you back. And for God's sake, stay safe. How 'bout I start you some divorce papers pronto, K? I'll take a look at the Wisconsin laws."

"That would be fantastic."

"Gotta bounce," Belinda said, and hung up.

Maddy sat at the table, idly petting Daisy's head for several minutes.

Exactly *why* had she cut Belinda out of her life? But she stopped her self-recriminations. She would not go there. She was moving forward every day, and now she had also righted a big wrong. A giant hole was filled.

She went into Ethel's house to say she was going for a run.

"Promise me you will let me know when you're back from your run, would you, dear?" Ethel asked. "Just for, you know, for the time being."

"I will. And it is just fine with me that you want that."

After a record-speed change into running clothes and getting the heck out of the casita, she and Daisy hit the trail behind the world-renowned observatory. As she ran through the ponderosa-pine woods, Maddy realized how great it was to have Ethel, Belinda, and perhaps Miles, on her safety team. And, of course, Daisy. Daisy would not let Arthur get near her.

"Would you, girl?"

But Daisy was already thirty feet ahead of her, nose to the ground, scouting for squirrels, rabbits, and deer.

Arthur's voice was still inside Maddy's mind, but it was fading. Fading fast. She ran and ran and ran.

Chapter 40

Miles stepped into the basement of the Weatherton Hotel. It would one day become a hipster bar, but for the moment it still served as simply a downtown place where you could get a cheap drink. Last month at the rally he'd been handed a notice for the meeting "Anti-Immigrant Information HERE". He wasn't sure how those gathered would feel about journalists, but the notice had been distributed, so here he was. He had come late on purpose—for a change—hoping tardiness would give him anonymity. He'd worn a ball cap and an old pair of glasses.

He need not have bothered, he realized. Everyone in the basement room was mesmerized by the tall guy standing in front of them, a can of beer in one hand and a microphone in the other. Nobody turned to look at Miles as he slipped in and leaned against the back wall.

"And unless we get control of these migrants sneaking over the Mexican border, our jobs may as well be dirt. And for God's sake, let's call them what they are: Illegal Aliens."

Miles watched the room's occupants enthusiastically nod their heads, murmuring their approval. He reminded himself that the people in the room—ninety-nine percent men though he saw the Carruthers woman from the protest, nearly all white—felt their livelihoods were at risk. He knew it was easy to blame people coming across the southern border. Recent arrivals to any country often bore the brunt of the blame from those just above them in social and economic status. The Irish arriving in Boston, the Chinese in California, of course the slaves arriving from Africa, and on and on. What an irony that it was only the white men who took over Native American lands—and condemning them to the Long Walk onto horrible reservation lands that nobody else wanted—that the new-comers ended up the ones in charge. Sometimes he felt guilty for just *being* a white guy.

He forced his attention back to the room, focusing on the speaker. The man had silver hair and—what were they—eerie eyes. Slightly unfocused, looking like they were about to roll back into the guy's head. Arctic blue—nearly the color of dry ice. He looked hipper than most of the men in the room who wore baggy jeans and plaid flannel shirts—the classic Flagstaff look. This guy was straight out of central casting for an outdoorsy film: stylish nylon pants of climbers and a button-down, zipping pockets, REI-type travel shirt. He finished his anti-immigrant sentiments and opened the floor for questions.

Miles recognized Stan Trumpet the shuttle man who stood up first. He also noted that sitting beside the shuttle driver was Harold Boyle, the other guy from the rally and the graveyard.

"You got everything right, Frank," Stan said, nodding. "Sure you did."

Miles jotted down "Frank". He'd need to get his last name as well.

"But you ain't said what we're supposed to *do* with all you talked about. I was at that damn rally last month, and I can stand here together with all of you"—his hand swept back toward the crowd of maybe two dozen people—"but that just ain't enough. We gotta make a plan, get us some *action* plan."

The room erupted in hollers and hoots. Miles wrote furiously but decided against taking out his audio recorder. Before Frank could answer, Miles was surprised to see Beez from the observatory stand up. Miles noticed his scratches had faded.

"Look, everybody," Beez started in his quiet voice that somehow made everyone else quiet down, too. "I agree that we gotta get this all better controlled. At the border, and also with the job-employment center where these guys show up to take our rightful jobs."

More nods and words of agreement from the crowd.

"But don't forget that some of the jobs they're takin' are ones we just don't want to do much ourselves. I'll admit I got me a good job, a real good job. Know I'm lucky about that. But tell the truth now—who wants to dig ditches in the hundred-degree heat down in that hellhole called Phoenix? Or clean up sewage leaks like the ones we get here sometimes? Maybe the darker-skinned guys, these illegals, don't believe they're too good to take this kinda work."

Miles was surprised that a few people nodded their agreement, but not a bit surprised that nobody clapped or cheered.

Frank spoke again.

"I'm not saying we want the shittiest of jobs, 'cause of course we don't. We got pride compared to those others. So I agree with what you had to say." He nodded toward Beez. "What I'm saying here is that there comes a time we need to stick up for our livelihoods, our lives, our very selves."

More cheers.

"And I agree with what your man Stan said: We got to get a plan. So let's talk more about that. But not when we have the press here with us."

He pointed at Miles, who raised his eyes to the guy called Frank and his notebook to the crowd. More than one man moved in his direction, and Miles wasn't sure if he should feel threatened or not. He decided he didn't.

"Hey, everybody. I'm Miles Harper, and I'm a reporter for the *Gazette.* That's our local paper, in case you're not from around here," he said, wondering how many of these folks were imported out-of-towners just here for this event. "I got word of your gathering and thought I'd come by and see what you all have to say. I like to think I'm the eyes and ears of the community. And that you might want to share your stories with me, with my readers."

Several people looked back at Frank, apparently hoping for direction. Frank gazed at the reporter for several seconds before speaking.

"We can't ban you from the meeting, Miles Harper, but you won't be hearing squat about anything further, so I suspect you may want to hightail it outta here."

Or what? Miles thought but didn't say.

"Sure, Frank. Can I get your last name, please?"

"Smith," Frank said after a beat. "Frank Smith." A few guys laughed.

"I'll leave a couple of my cards on this back table, in case anybody wants to talk to me more," Miles said.

He wondered what this Frank guy would get out of faking his last name, which he obviously had. "Remember, folks, it's your newspaper, too, and you all have a chance to share your voice, your opinions with the public. And Mr. *Smith*, there's a card here for you, too."

Outside, Miles stood on the corner of Aspen Avenue and Leroux Street, wondering if anyone would come outside to meet him. After several minutes, he realized nobody was going to talk with him in such a public way. He hoped he would get a call, though.

He really wanted to know more about their action plan. A whole lot more.

Chapter 41

Luis Ortega stood in front of a different crowd a week later, waiting for people to settle in. He knew they were afraid. He knew how much they wanted answers. He wanted answers, too. He also felt afraid, but for different reasons. Residents were afraid of a serial killer and what that meant for their families in this town where they had always felt safe. Of course, he was also concerned for this town he had always worked to keep safe. But his main fear stemmed from his inability to solve the murders yet. Luis was afraid he would fail his hometown.

He would not share all that with the crowd, but he could be transparent in what he knew, and what they could do to try—*try*—to keep themselves safe during this time. But he also knew he could not guarantee anyone's safety. He felt the eyes of his father from the back row as Luis addressed the people of Flagstaff.

"Thanks for coming out," he started, looking at the mothers, fathers, kids, and neighbors, many he had known since childhood, some he had met as a younger adult, and some he did not recognize. Flagstaff had changed over the past decade or two, and he was always surprised when he went to a restaurant or shopping and saw not one person he knew. What was happening to his town?

He stood in the high school auditorium. He had

predicted—correctly—that the turnout would be high, and the police station conference room would not be large enough. Ortega could hear the sounds of dribbling basketballs and squeaking sneakers from down the hall, and he realized that some in the crowd were on their way to see their children play ball afterwards.

"While I do not have a lot to say beyond what you may have read or heard in the press, I want to bring you up to date on our investigation," he said. He saw Miles slipping into an aisle seat in the back of the room, pen soon flying over a notepad. Phoenix news cameras were there, and a couple of other reporters from the larger metro area, and a local blogger. He hated that this story was drawing so much coverage, but how could it not?

While people were killed in northern Arizona on a regular basis, especially in some rural areas related to alcohol-fueled domestic violence, it was unusual to have someone murdered at the observatory. He grimaced internally. *Was it the fame of the place that brought the reporters? Or the fact that two people were dead in just over a month's time in this little city/large town? My town.*

He reported what he knew of the victims, and the early morning hours of the killings.

"Everyone—all of you—should be particularly alert at that time of the day. If you work the late-night shift, please leave work in pairs or teams, if possible. Any questions?"

"Should we be afraid in our own homes, Luis?" asked an older woman whom he had known since he was a boy.

"I do not believe so, Mrs. Garcia," he answered cautiously. "That said, it's a good idea to start locking your doors at night. Even during the day. That's always best practice."

Miles raised his hand, and Luis nodded at him.

"How significant is it that both of these victims were working in those early hours of the day, and both were cleaners?"

A murmur moved through the crowd.

It irritated Ortega that Miles would ask this publicly when he had so much access to Ortega privately, but he did not allow his emotions to show.

"They were *both* cleaners?" asked a tall man in the back. His long face was very white, and Luis saw faded pink scratches on his cheeks. This must be the guy from the observatory, who Miles had alerted him about. Beasley, was it?

"Yes they were," Luis answered, making a mental note to follow up on the man's identity, which he had not yet done. "Both were young people who rather recently moved to Flagstaff. They were helping their family cleaning businesses."

"Illegal immigrants?" called out another white man. Luis nodded toward one of his men, mentally ordering him to get this man's ID, too. He had to be careful not to turn the case into one of racism, just because he himself was a Latino. Still, could it be a coincidence that both vics were minorities?

"No, neither were that we know of," Luis answered. Their investigation had not yet answered that question regarding the Mexican victim, but he should be hearing back from ICE—U.S. Immigration and Customs Enforcement—very soon. The agency was backlogged and was months behind its normal deadlines.

"And how sure are you that the killer is not sitting in this room, looking for his next victim?" asked the man with the scratches.

"We do not," Luis conceded. "But I can tell you everyone in this room is a potential target of the killer—or killers—and a potential suspect."

He wished he could take away those words as soon as they had left his mouth. Too dramatic, he realized. The situation called for calm and care, not drama. He avoided looking at his father.

"Do you think these were done by more than one murderer?" asked a Phoenix TV reporter. "Or more than one perp at both the killing scenes?"

"We do not know the answer to that yet," Luis said, noting how television reporters in particular loved words like "perp" and "killing scene." "We are looking at all evidence that could yield that answer."

With that, he told everyone in the room to keep their eyes open, to report any suspicious activity, or any little thing out of the ordinary that they noticed that might help.

"I would rather you phone our dispatchers twice a day than not make a call until it's too late," he said. On the whiteboard behind him he wrote the phone number of an anonymous police tip line and his cell phone number, assuring them that he would personally answer any call. After that, he ended the meeting.

A few people came up to ask him more questions, while his father waited until they were gone.

"You did well, son," Luis Ortega Sr. assured him. "Good balance of alerting them to the dangers and telling them what they could do. I would not be surprised if some folks contacted you soon about something they know."

"I should not have been so dramatic," Luis criticized himself as the two Ortegas walked out of the building together.

"Murder is dramatic," his father said. "*Muy dramatico*."

Chapter 42

Harold Boyle woke up on the hard ground up behind Mars Hill. He'd seen a few camouflaged tents in the woods, so figured it was an okay spot to spend the night. He pulled his sleeping bag up to his chin against the cool dawn air. He turned onto his side and slept lightly for another hour.

Boyle knew everyone in Flagstaff was talking about the recent murders. A night-shift worker at the observatory and then one at a Route 66 motel. *Who would do this*, he knew they were asking? He tried to get into the headspace of the coppers. Were they on the trail of the murderer? Would they be making an arrest soon? That guy Stan at the immigration protest seemed pretty explosive. When Harold had asked him if he wanted to get a coffee after they talked to that reporter at the park, the guy had started yelling.

"Why would I go for coffee with a total stranger?" Stan had shouted. So Harold had just shrugged and turned to go when the jerk called out to him.

"Look, forget it," Stan had said, walking over and leaning down due to their height difference. "I can fly off the handle for no reason. I know it ain't right."

The guy's anger seemed to come and go at random. But then that morning after the cemetery when they had breakfast, he seemed pretty normal.

It wasn't the guy's words that were offensive, he

thought now, walking down the hill toward the Greyhound station. *It was more the violence hidden beneath the random words.* Boyle wondered if the coppers were looking at Stan.

Were any of the guys camping out in the local woods in danger? Was he? It was only a matter of time.

Harold shoved the bus ticket into his back pocket and stepped inside the men's room. Bus station toilets were always a better bet than waiting for someone to get out of the bus's cramped ones. He looked in the mirror and liked what he saw. A healthier him. His face had a bit more color since he'd been back in Flagstaff—things were going pretty good.

After getting paid by the observatory and the old lady, he was ready to make some changes. He needed to go back to California and close up his mother's house, then he'd come back here and find a decent place to live, maybe a rooming house for starters, and settle in. He wasn't one for self-reflection, but as he literally looked at himself, he knew he was seriously back on top.

He stepped out of the washroom and checked for his bus. Not in from Albuquerque yet. He'd wait outside where he could have a smoke.

Yep, he was on his way up. He wished he could tell his mother about it, but that was no longer possible. Still, he knew she was probably watching him from some place. Above or below, he couldn't say for sure.

Chapter 43

Junior "Freddie Fly" Begay was working the late shift. He still washed cars three days a week at the quick-mart carwash across Milton Road from the university, but this fall he was promoted to part-time cashier as well. He didn't mind soaping up cars some days and working the register both the day and night shifts He always liked talking to people. Helped with the tips, sure, for his long-term plan, but it mostly made the time fly by. Plus, he genuinely liked people.

"You're not the stereotype stone-faced Indian brave," his mother told him once when he couldn't have been more than eight years old. "From the time you were in your cradle board, you were always smiling, and trying to get out—mostly so you could go around hugging everyone. You're my social monarch butterfly, and you stay proud of that, Freddie Fly."

She had died the very next year. She'd always called him Freddie Fly after a monarch butterfly, while his dad and sisters and brothers referred to him as Junior, since his father was Fred Begay Sr. The "Junior" nickname had stuck during middle and high school, but he always introduced himself to new people as Freddie Fly. He'd finally gotten a couple of his closest pals and his on-again off-again girlfriend Sheila to call him Freddie. When he moved to L.A., he planned to only respond to Freddie Fly, and, that way, it would be like taking his mother along to the big city.

Both of his parents were passed now. Most of his siblings—the ones who left the Rez—were living in Albuquerque, and one sister was in Los Angeles. He was saving to move in with that sister, Betty, in L.A., who recently had her second baby and could use some help with childcare. Plus, she admitted she felt a little lost in the city, and she missed him.

She and her husband Leonard both wanted him to come.

"If you save up $1,000, you can come live with us, Junior," Leonard told him on a Skype call, his sister nodding in the background as she sat with their kids on her lap. "That's just so you have some cash on hand when you arrive. I wouldn't want you to come broke, and we all get off to a bad start."

"Put it in a real bank, little bro," Betty had advised him.

He liked his brother-in-law and adored Betty. He had nearly $900 saved up now from all the overtime—and had actually opened a bank account instead of keeping it under his mattress like all his friends did. Yeah, he was almost ready for The City of Angels! He'd quit drinking and smoking—anything—three months ago. Man, had that saved him some dough. He'da been a millionaire if he'd done that at sixteen instead of eighteen!

"Woulda been a millionaire," he said aloud as he gave a couple of teenagers their change for their orange pops.

"Huh?" one of them asked.

"Oh, sorry. Day dreamin'. Caught me out talkin' to myself."

"My uncle does that all day," the boy answered, rolling his eyes but smiling.

Both kids had some stellar ink jobs, and Freddie told them so.

They inspected the raven perched on his bicep and compared notes on who was the best tat artist in town.

"Go slow, now," he told them, sounding like an old man.

"Later," they said in unison and walked out, the bell above the door ding-a-linging behind them.

Freddie was just about to close up the register when the bell jingled again. A guy—or was it a skinny woman, he couldn't tell—came in. The person looked kinda familiar. White hoodie, baggie jeans but the old man's kind, not the rapper kind, plus some splotchy skin peeking from inside the hoodie. Freddie realized he'd seen the person hanging around the carwash/gas station over the past couple of weeks. Maybe homeless, he decided. He could sure sympathize, what with the economy flat as the distant mesas behind his childhood home.

He let the bum wander through the aisles, half watching for shoplifting, half wondering what he'd do if the guy—or woman—grabbed something. A candy bar or chips going out the door, Freddie would look the other way. A six-pack, though, and he'd have to make a move. He felt in his jeans pocket and fingered the spare coins and a couple of bucks. Maybe he'd give it to the brother or sister, act like he got the change wrong, to protect their pride.

He really wanted to close up. It was close to eleven. Sheila had called him to ask when he got off work. He needed to tell her about his plans to move to

Cali. She wouldn't be happy, he was pretty sure, but at least it would no longer be weighing on him. He didn't want to lead her on. When they weren't arguing about dumb stuff, they really made each other laugh. But since he'd gone "all sober" on her, she said he wasn't near as much fun. He was okay with that.

He heard the slapping of sneakered feet. What the hell! Hoodie was running right at Freddie. He was coming for the counter. He had something shiny in his hand. What was happening!?! The bilagáana *was jumping the counter. With a knife!*

Oh my God, the pain in his arm. Freddie managed to grab the bat behind the counter and hit back, but his arm was so tired, so very tired. He reached for the alarm buzzer that his boss said he'd never need but was good to know about, and then everything went black.

But, oh, the pain. The pain was red.

Chapter 44

Miles was out of bed and on his bicycle, bike-light shining, five minutes after hearing the police-radio traffic just before midnight.

"10-33," the scanner squawked again, from his backpack this time. An officer was calling in an emergency, requesting backup.

"10-39," he heard, as fellow officers reported that they were on their way.

The address was on South Milton Road, the 900 block, but Miles couldn't place the business. He thought it might be near the Motel 8 where they'd arrested the drunk guy.

"Don't let it be another murder," he said into the night air as he pedaled under the railroad bridge and onto Milton Road. "Don't let somebody else be dead."

He turned into the driveway of the carwash right next door to the motel—the same lot where Maddy had parked her car during the motel-arrest incident, and where he'd gotten coffee just last month. A half dozen cop cars clogged the parking lot, along with two ambulances. One of those had its back doors opened, and EMTs were loading a stretcher with a body into the vehicle. Miles could see the blanket was soaked with blood. Doors slammed, and the ambulance careened out of the lot going north on Milton toward the hospital, sirens screaming. So the victim was probably still alive.

He saw a female cop standing with a small woman, a girl really, who was leaning on the back of a beat-up pickup and crying. Sobbing. Long raven-black hair cascaded over her face and arms, her clothing a bloodied mess.

Other officers were inside the carwash/convenience store, their dark uniforms practically shining under the fluorescent lighting. Miles spotted Ortega talking to one of the cops outside the convenience store and hurried over.

"You got here in a jiffy," Ortega said, gum popping. "Sleeping with your scanner again?"

"You know it. What the hell happened?"

Miles and Luis watched the officer help the young Native American woman into the back of a squad car and then slide in beside her. Another cop was behind the wheel, and they drove off, no sirens. As the car drove past, Miles saw tree leaves of ink on the girl's neck.

"Hey, I've seen her before," he said.

"Name's Sheila Manygoats. When did you see her? And where?"

"The day you made the arrest of the intoxicated guy," Miles said, nodding toward the adjacent motel. "She was at the gas station—right over there—when Maddy and I left."

"Sure?"

"That tattoo. No question."

Ortega unclipped his radio mouthpiece from his jacket and passed on Miles's information to the dispatcher.

"Who is she?" Miles asked, pulling out his notebook. "And who's the victim in the ambulance?"

"Sheila Manygoats says she's the victim's girlfriend. His name's Fred Begay, goes by Junior or Freddie, she said. Through tears that seemed very real."

"She looked wrecked."

"Said she was supposed to meet the vic after he closed up. Swears that as she was approaching the store she saw someone running off. She could not say if it was a man or woman. Very convenient. Blood everywhere behind the counter and all over her. Maybe she is in shock, or maybe she just knifed her boyfriend."

"Poor gal."

"She has no record. No petty crimes. Completely clean. Same with him, except an under-age drinking charge about three years ago."

"Dead?"

"Pretty much almost."

"Alive?"

"Pretty much almost."

Miles wrote quickly to keep up, in his personal shorthand. He'd get a formal quote from Luis on his recorder before he left.

"If he was working behind the counter, I may know that kid," Miles said.

"Yeah?"

"Not know him, know him. I mean I've met him. Got a coffee here not long ago. That day the angry shuttle driver Stan Trumpet was getting gas and cigarettes. He, Stan, had a mild confrontation with a mom who was trying to get him to move the shuttle so she could get gas.

"Get to the point, Miles."

"Well, the kid kind of tried to stick up for her, and

the guy Stan did not like that."

"The kid, was he angry, too?"

"Not really. He was just trying to keep the peace."

"Okay, try to remember every detail of that incident. And we can talk more tomorrow."

"Right. Any other witnesses besides the girl?"

"Not yet. But we cannot ignore all that blood on her."

"Right."

"Like that TV show *The Fugitive.* The man blames his wife's murder on the damn one-armed man," Ortega said. "My father always said that show was a classic case of the real perpetrator creating a distraction. A good story—but one that was too damn good to believe. As in, the bastard killed his own wife."

Miles recalled watching reruns of *The Fugitive* with his parents and sisters when he was probably too young for the show, though his nonstop begging finally wore his folks down. It had always scared the hell out of him, serving up nightmares every time. The main thing he remembered was that the main character wasn't guilty.

"But the fugitive was innocent," Miles said.

"So he claimed, Miles. So he claimed."

Chapter 45

Stan Trumpet loaded up his Ford F-250 for the drive back home.

East Texas, here I come, he thought, with no affection.

He'd told his boss at Arizona Shuttle that he had a family emergency, but of course that wasn't exactly true. He needed to get out town for a while, a good long while. Ever since the newspaper man came to the rally and then the meeting in that downtown basement, Stan had been on guard. Because he'd seen the fake-news guy talking with that Mexican cop over at the cemetery. Then he and that Boyle had been interviewed—first by the law and then by that reporter who followed them into Benny's. And Stan had just gotten a voice message from the police detective to come to the station for another fuckin' interview. Ha! As if.

Everything felt too close for comfort. With his history, they'd be onto him like jelly on a pb&j sandwich. He wasn't about to stay put. He was pretty sure Boyle suspected Stan had something to do with the murders. He wasn't about to stick around to find out.

Not that he ever loved going back to the Lone Star State, but at least it was familiar, and safe, for the moment anyway.

From where Trumpet sat, both murders sounded a lot like drug deals gone bad—at least he hoped it sounded like that to law enforcement. And ain't he heard from that horse-face Beez, was it, that there were drugs at the observatory? And the young East Indian at the motel sure coulda been a low-level dealer. Because after the downtown meeting, that Frank-man—who everyone knew dealt drugs—made a comment about the motel killing.

Stan wasn't supposed to hear it, but he was standing outside smoking a cig when Frank and some other anti-immigrants were inside the bar, talking, the basement window wide open for the whole downtown to hear.

"I heard that motel boy was here illegally," one of the guys said.

"I don't know about that," Frank had answered. Stan recognized his smooth voice. "But he was running drugs, and not doing a very good job."

Stan didn't know what all that meant, except that if he left town, maybe the cops would lower him as a priority suspect and follow some other leads—for a while, anyway. And maybe they'd think it all had to do with drugs.

And Frank-man. The drug dealer who hated illegals as much as Stan did.

He looked at the various flyers he'd been circulating for Icy Eyes.

"Stop the Invasion!" and "Go Home or Face the Consequences!" and "We're Watching You!"

He pulled into a gas station and dumped nearly the lot of them. Not a good idea to have them as evidence. Still, he kept one, shoving it deep under his seat, a souvenir of his time in Arizona. He figured he was done with this state. Lots of other places to go in the United

States of America. After hiding out in home sweet home.

Now he was on I-40, headed east. He hoped nobody would track him to his hometown any time soon.

I ain't waiting around to find out.

Chapter 46

Charlie was crying. Sobbing. And scrubbing.

She grasped the vegetable-scouring brush in her right hand and forced the bristles under her left-hand fingernails, scraping it back and forth, back and forth, then switching hands to repeat.

Who could guess how difficult it was to get blood out from underneath your nails?

She replayed the scene over and over in her head, as she worked to eliminate the bloodstains from her hands. She would attack her shirt and pants next. Actually, she knew there was no saving them.

How had she gotten in so deep? When had she tumbled over the edge, beyond that of which she thought herself capable? Sure, she had become a recreational user. She told herself she just needed something to give her a release from her job pressures, her life pressures. But the dealing? How had she even let that happen? And the violence that came with it? Would she ever be able to rid herself of her scary dealer?

What kind of guy calls himself Frank-man? I mean, really.

She scrubbed and scrubbed, salty tears melting into the faucet water. She was pretty sure Luis Ortega had been watching her closely. That could only mean one thing. She was a suspect.

She had to come up with a plan. A plan for her future. Was her life going to end up a disaster—with no hope? Would the negative headlines be about her this time, instead of her writing about others, like back in the day? She longed to call her mother.

But you can't call a person who's dead.

Chapter 47

Miles sat hunched over his keyboard, typing his latest speculations on the killings. It was nearly two a.m.

He had the newsroom—the entire building—all to himself. He felt safely ensconced by the emptiness, the uncommon lack of human conversation. His radio was turned to KUYI 88.1 FM, the Native American Public Radio Station broadcast from the Hopi Reservation. It played an eclectic mixture of Native music, local announcements like weekend potlucks and sheep for sale, and even oldies rock 'n roll. Miles loved the mix.

Not something you'd find back in Chicago. Am I a lucky dude, or what?

There was also the buzz of the fluorescent lights overhead, and the occasional passing of a vehicle out front. And the light tapping of his computer keys—so much quieter than the back-in-the-day sound of typewriters. That clacking of the electric typewriters had been a soothing, familiar sound over the years, but it hadn't been all that long before he'd become used to the quieter computer keyboards. Now the thought of using a typewriter in the profession was antiquated, but he still remembered fondly the clicking and clacking of the newsrooms in those days that seemed so much simpler.

He texted Ruthless that he had a front-page story

on the most recent theories about the killings, adding that he was in the office now.

Within seconds, he heard the sound of a train whistle—not an actual train but his text-message alert: Ruth.

—Can't sleep. Be in soon. Left keys at wrk. Unlock door. CU.—

Miles grinned. Maybe some of his own organization skills—or lack thereof—were rubbing off on his boss. He would really give her hell when she arrived.

He walked through the mostly dark building and opened the press-room door to see snow spitting, though nothing much was sticking to the dirt parking lot. He closed it again, double checked that it was unlocked, and texted Ruth.

—Press room entrance open.—

Back at his desk, his fingers flew over the keyboard, while his mind worked almost independently on the unsolved murders. He looked absently at the note Butch had left him. Haphazard as ever.

"Dude came in again, wearing a whatchacallit. Oh, said he'd be back soon. Left you this note. C u nxt wk. Butch."

But which dude, and what the hell was the "whatchacallit"? Butch was off and not answering his cell.

Now that was familiar, Miles thought sheepishly.

Miles unfolded the half-crumpled page of lined paper, as if someone had been carrying it around for a while. He read the words scrawled on the page.

"Ready to talk? H Bates"

Who the heck was H Bates? Maybe this guy just

was somebody who saw something at one of the murder scenes.

Miles knew he'd blown it by not making a point to get into the newspaper lobby quickly enough to meet this man Bates. He sure would talk to him when he came back to the paper.

His thoughts turned to the Native carwash kid Freddie Junior. He wondered if he would survive. He remembered liking him that day he bought his newspaper and coffee. The guy had remained chill, given the pressure he was under from the furious shuttle driver. Those thoughts brought him around to Stan. Ortega had told him Stan had just left town and that Stan's boss had said he'd left for a family emergency. For real, or the perfect excuse to disappear?

Then there was Charlie. She *had* been acting strangely and was looking like she was hooked on some kind of drugs. Still, Miles couldn't see her getting blood on her hands. But then, he really didn't know her that well. Not anymore.

He stopped, mid-thoughts, and pulled out his notebook, flipping through the pages. According to both autopsies, the person who stabbed the victims used his (or her) right hand. All the suspects were right-handed, Ortega had said, though Miles wasn't sure how the detective knew that. *Let's assume that much was true,* Miles thought. *But wasn't there a different issue with the stab wounds?*

Snap! Stan was extremely tall, ditto on Beez, and Charlie was short, Tanak, too. He thought back to what Butch had first told him about the visitor.

"Not tall, not short." Hadn't he said in that frustrating way of his? Maybe not so frustrating!

According to what the M.E. reported—inexplicably nearly hidden in a footnote—the knife was inserted into the bodies of both victims at a straight angle. Meaning, Miles was pretty sure, the killer was about the same height as the two victims—one who was about five feet six inches and the other five feet eight inches. Was this true, or just his fired-up imaginings based on reading hundreds of mystery novels?

He clicked his way through sites on the Internet, and there it was. "Using Knife Angle Entering the Body Wound to Estimate a Knife-wielder's Height," by a researcher at a western university. *What did we do before the Internet anyway?* He glanced through the scholarly article—glad he never had to use the stuffy language found in academic journals—and turned back to his own writing. He was on a roll.

"One double sweet roll, coming up," he joked to the newsroom. No response.

He stopped typing and searched his notes again, finally finding what Ortega had told him the last time they compared notes.

"Our officers cleared Boyle after he purchased a ticket and boarded a west-bound bus before the Fred Begay Jr. incident," Ortega had told him. His notes also reminded Miles that Luis said Stan had apparently gone to Texas *after* the latest murder attempt. And that he had alerted Texas about Trumpet's possible role in the stabbings. So maybe it was Stan the van man. But still. Something was off. His notes ended.

Miles thought about the mystery man who had stopped by the paper at least three times. Butch's initial vague description was actually similar to one of the men at the anti-immigration rally and basement meeting, Miles realized now. When he checked the dates on his notes, he saw that the guy who had come by the newspaper to see him—now it seemed it was one H Bates—was there the day *after* the killings. And again today.

Boyle. Harold Boyle, who was a lot shorter than both Stan the Man or Beez. And taller than Charlie. *But then who's this H Bates?* He'd just have to wait until the man returned.

Miles's mind was spinning like bicycle wheels on a summer day. What if Boyle never did get on that bus? Did the cops actually *see* him board via the surveillance footage? Was Harold Boyle in cahoots with H Bates?

"Reading Tony Hillerman mysteries does not make you a detective," Luis had admonished him just the other day. Still.

He called Ortega but reached his voicemail, so he texted the detective.

—Got something—the angle of the stabbings; and timing. Call me! At Gaz—

Miles wondered if somebody would ever invent a faster way to text. Instead of the aaa, bbb, ccc hunt-and-peck method, which could seriously drive a guy nuts.

As he finished texting, Miles heard Ruth's footsteps coming through the building and looked behind him at the newsroom entrance. It would be good to have her as a sounding board. He turned back to his computer, his mind replaying everything he'd been working out.

He saw Ruth's milky reflection on his computer screen. *Wearing a hoodie, not very Ruth-like*, he thought. *Come to think of it, where was that distinct sound of her clicking heels?*

"'Bout time you came to work, you slacker," he joked, swiveling in his chair.

His editor was not wearing a hoodie, standing in the doorway. It was Harold Boyle, pale lips curving slightly upward.

"So, mister big-shot reporter fake-news man," Boyle said in a raspy voice. "Came to your newspaper, ready to give you clues, but you were too damn busy."

Boyle walked toward Miles, pulling a knife from the pocket of his red hoodie.

Miles made it to behind the adjacent desk just in time. Now the desks were between the men.

He's going to kill me because I didn't interview him? wondered Miles, incredulous. *And, wait, was he Harold Boyle or H Bates?*

"Look, man. I'm sorry I didn't take the time to sit down and talk with you. I was busy," he said, working to keep his face neutral and the fear out of his voice. "And you know why? *You.* You were keeping me busy with those murders. I'm here late at night to file yet one more story on *you*, on your killing spree."

"You think I'd really stab you because you ignored me? Ha!"

His laugh was bitter, his voice cracking.

Miles estimated that Boyle was about five feet eight.

Not tall, not short.

"No. You're the only person who could point the finger at me. First, you knew I was still in Flagstaff after I killed that foreign, rotten singer at the motel on Route 66. Cuz you saw me at the carwash watching the coppers take down the drunk not long after."

Miles wondered about this. Boyle had been at the

basement meeting and the cemetery after the killing of Rafat. So he wasn't making all that much sense.

"Second, I left you a message today. Course wasn't sure if that lazy bastard would get it to you or not. Guy's a piece'a work. But I realized I shouldn't've given you more proof I was in Flagstaff for the final killing. Of that not-so-brave Indian. When I saw the lights on tonight, I knew I was supposed to come in."

The newsroom lights reflected off the long knife in his hand. His right hand. Two metal desks still divided the men.

"Wait, Boyle," Miles said, standing on legs that suddenly trembled like aspen leaves. He again tried to calm his voice.

"Too late*, bro,*" Boyle said. "Now it's your turn. Your turn to *die.*"

Isn't that a James Bond film? Miles wondered crazily. *No, wait. "No Time to Die". Sure like that title better!*

He backed away, reaching for the desk phone, but Boyle grabbed the phone cord, slicing it with his knife as easily as a chain saw through Swiss cheese. *Or a human being.* Miles swallowed. He held his cell phone behind his back, and pushed what he hoped was the redial button, letting his phone fall onto the newsroom floor as he cranked up HOPI radio to cover the sound of the phone dropping. The room was filled with Hopi men chanting, and Boyle stopped in his tracks, unnerved.

"Shut them up!" he screamed, lunging. Miles threw the desk phone at Boyle, barely grazing the killer's forehead. But Boyle clutched the knife more tightly, and came at Miles, shoving the first desk aside so he could just barely stand between the two desks.

Miles kept backing up. Only one desk between them now. After reading hundreds of mysteries, Miles believed by keeping the killer talking he might save himself.

"Look, before you kill me, what do you mean I saw you? Where were you?"

"I was right there watching the coppers arrest the drunk. Of course, you didn't notice me. Not too observant for a reporter. Or should I say, not too smart?"

Miles wracked his brain, recreating the people at the carwash adjacent to the motel where he and Maddy had huddled behind the police car with Luis. Snap! *The guy in the dark hoodie! Standing with the other curious bystanders—including the most recent victim's girlfriend with the neck tattoo.*

"Just tell me what happened," Miles said, hoping his voice sounded level but curious. "Why did you kill those people. What did they ever do to you?"

Miles thought that if he could just jump over both desks at an angle, he could outrun Boyle to the back door. That was a big "if" though.

He felt the handlebars of his bike push into him from behind and knew his back was up against the wall—literally.

Boyle stood stock still on the other side of the desk, as if suspended in time.

"And I could tell your story now, from your point of view. Before you, you know, stab me."

Not if I can help it.

"You know why you're still alive, asshole?"

"No."

Miles reached behind him, clutching the handlebars with one hand and bike seat with the other.

"Because I wanted you to see me before you died," Boyle said, his eyes glaring, voice cracking again. "I wanted you to know you were gonna die. Never thought I'd kill a white man, but then again, it would have to be a flaming liberal like your sorry bleeding-heart white ass. And there's always a first time for everything, my mother used to tell me. Boy, she got that right in the end! Ha!"

Boyle jumped onto the empty desk. Miles yanked the bike out from behind him, distantly thinking how smart he was to have brought his bike inside the office tonight. He caught Boyle in the ribs—hard—with the rear wheel. Boyle slipped and fell off the desk, the knife clattering onto the floor. Miles raised his bike up again. This time he brought the handlebars of his sweet ride down on the killer's face.

Miles didn't stop to see if Boyle was getting up. He snagged his phone, scrambled over the two desks, and ran as fast as he could toward the back of the building, hoping against hope that he'd make it outside before the murderer caught up with him. He gave silent thanks to Ruth's ultimatum to clean off his desk, without which he would surely have slipped on the mess, impeding his escape.

He was three steps from the back door when it flew open and Ruth walked in, the click, click, click of her heels accompanying her.

He heard the footsteps behind them, and grabbed his boss, sweeping her off her feet without sparing energy on words.

"Miles, what the hell—"

He threw her over his shoulder, fireman style, and ran outside and to the street, turning northeast toward downtown. Ruth was not as light as he thought she would be, and he was no weightlifter, but he kept going.

"Put me down, Miles! Are you *drunk*?" Ruth demanded, squirming to get free and throwing him off balance.

He heard distant sirens.

"Killer," he wheezed. "In the building,"

"Put me down, you idiot. I can run faster than this."

He dropped her to the ground and looked back into the night. No more sound of footsteps, and he couldn't see anyone following them.

Ruth kicked off her heels—lime green tonight—and they ran onto the narrow wooden bridge over the dry Rio de Flag beside the public library. Still no Boyle. She pulled out her cell phone and tapped at it with her bright green fingernails. Miles leaned on his knees, gasping for air, in the middle of Wheeler Park. A couple of people lying on park benches raised their heads to look at the odd couple, then went back to sleep.

Before Ruth reached the police dispatcher, a half dozen cop cars raced past the park, toward the newspaper building.

Miles's cell rang. Ortega.

"I'm in Wheeler Park," Miles told him between breaths. "Boyle's the killer. He just tried to stab me in the newsroom. Not sure where he is now."

He listened for several seconds, hung up, put the phone in its holster, and looked at Ruth.

"He said to stay put until he texts me or when a

squad car shows up."

Ruth retrieved her bright shoes from the other side of the bridge, and they waited in the library parking lot.

"Am I still fired?" Miles asked, his heart still beating hard.

"You're off probation—at least for now," she said. "But you definitely owe me a new pair of panty hose."

Ortega texted Miles to return to the newspaper office. When they arrived, the detective stood outside talking with an officer who then walked into the building.

"Heard you and the killer on my cell—and somebody chanting?" Ortega said, talking to Miles as he nodded hello to Ruth. "I hung up, called backup, and came over. What the hell?"

"Hopi radio."

"You okay, Ruth?" Ortega asked.

"Miles got me out of there—barely," she said. "I'd only just arrived when he grabbed me and carried me over to the library. Carried me like a damn fireman, for God's sake. Thought I was gonna have to do fuckin' mouth-to-mouth on the kid, he was breathing so bad by the time we stopped running."

Ortega snorted a laugh.

Badly, Miles thought, but didn't say. He'd only just got off probation, after all.

Miles filled them in on what he had put together about the killings right before Boyle showed up in the newsroom, and what the murderer had said.

Ortega said he had been sifting through his own notes and coming to basically the same conclusion. The person who had inputted the official information on the murders for the medical examiner had pretty much buried the information on the angles of the knife wounds. Once he had discovered that, the puzzle pieces fell together. In fact, he'd only missed Miles's call because he'd been on the phone, bouncing his theory off his father when he clicked on the M.E. footnote Miles had also found. By the time he saw Miles's text, he'd received the strange phone call with the chanting Hopis.

A little less than an hour later, the cops had cleared the building, and after agreeing to come into the police station later that day to make formal statements, Miles and Ruth had the place to themselves. It was nearly four in the morning.

"You solved the case, paper boy," Ruth said. "Redo your lead, and I'll look over what you'd written by the time that mad man showed up. I'll text Lisha to come in and help out. Jesus, what a fuckin' night."

A half hour later, Lisha came in, looking fresh and ready for the day.

"Man, he almost got you," she said to Miles, having heard the details from Ruth. "I would have been upset to lose you after knowing you such a short time."

Miles looked up from his computer, hearing something off in her voice.

"The truth is, Miles, while it would have been sad for you to be dead," she continued sweetly, brown eyes sparkling, "I probably would have received a raise to cover your job and mine until they found someone new."

Lisha grinned at him as she settled into her desk chair and turned on her computer.

"Too soon?" she asked, suddenly looking concerned.

"That's okay," Miles said. "Just glad to know where I stand with you."

They both cracked up, and even Ruthless joined in, a bit of the night's tension released.

Miles felt the last few hours sinking in. His arms ached—from carrying Ruth, yes, but also from using his bike as a weapon of self-defense. And from the gallons of adrenalin that had flowed through his body. Also, he was dead tired. *Better dead tired than dead dead,* he reflected grimly.

He felt like kissing his trusty mountain bike but instead examined it for damage. A few spots of dried blood marked the handlebar tape. Funny, he always locked his bike up outside, but tonight for no good reason he'd brought it into the office, propping it up behind him. *The choices we make,* he thought.

And then, what the hell, he did kiss the bicycle, but not on the handlebars, which he realized he'd better let the cops examine for Boyle's DNA, in case a match popped up on the National DNA Index System used by law enforcement agencies across the country.

Ruth and Lisha saw the kiss but, amazingly, both kept their mouths shut.

Suddenly, he looked forward to telling Maddy about the crazy night. But first, it was time to get this story done.

He leaned his sweet wheels back against the wall and began to type.

He hoped Boyle was long gone, and not about to make a victim of somebody else.

Chapter 48

Just before four a.m., Maddy left the warehouse with two other Caboose Coffee employees. They said their goodbyes, and she climbed into her Subarubie as the others drove out of the parking lot. The night was bathed in moonlight, and a light snow fell. It was early December.

She was tired but happy. She had frosted four dozen lemon scones, two dozen chocolate-chip scones, and three dozen gingerbread men—or rather ginger persons—cookies. Those were the most fun because she could draw on their faces with the sweet stuff. She had learned the recipes for the frosting—only three ingredients so not difficult—as well as the recipes for the cookies and scones and had enjoyed the quiet camaraderie of the late night/early morning shift. She found it meditative. Her dark, pre-Flagstaff life was a distant memory. Sure, she had been afraid after Arthur's arrival on the scene just last month. But according to Detective Ortega, it would be unusual for him to travel nearly 1,000 miles again when she now had a protective order out against him. The Milwaukee police had told Ortega that they had met with Dempster, and he appeared to understand the consequences of violating the order.

"I am so over it, and over her," he was quoted. "I was out of my mind. I realize that."

"I feel alive," she whispered into the chilly early morning. Then she yelled through her open window. "I am back!" she shouted into the air outside.

Out of the blue, she recalled Miles's crazy yodeling the day they met. Her windows still open, she yodeled at the top of her lungs.

Happy, she turned the key, and her lovely car jumped alive, too. But wait. Was that a shadow moving in the dark near the warehouse? Maybe she just imagined it. Thinking about the late-night killings now, she closed her windows and locked her doors, and backed up—fast—to get away from the warehouse. Cranking up the defroster, she decided not to get out and scrape the front windshield. A small rectangle was clearing on the glass, and she peered into the rearview mirror. Nothing there that she could see.

Switching quickly from peaceful calm to full fight-or-flight mode now, she pressed down on the gas pedal before she could even see all that well. By the time she got to the road, though, the windshield was two-thirds clear and Maddy took a big breath.

A few minutes later, headlights shined behind her, coming closer. Was someone following her from the Caboose Coffee parking lot? She drove through town, glancing from the road to her rearview mirror and back again. Someone was *definitely* following her. Or were they? When she slowed down even a bit, the car behind her did, too. When she sped up, there they were, practically on her bumper. It was too dark to see the driver.

After close to ten minutes, Maddy detoured to the large city/county building that housed the police station, sheriff's office, and county jail. As she turned into the parking lot, she watched the headlights melt away into the night.

She sat in front of the law-enforcement building for several minutes, feeling her heart rate slow. She considered going into the building and talking to someone on duty. But what would she say? *Someone was following me on the road? I saw a shadow and then a car was behind me?*

No, she would go home and if she still felt afraid, she would find Detective Ortega's card and give him a call. He had said to call any time. Probably did not mean at four a.m. because there was another car on the road, but still. If in fact the murderer was looking for late-night victims, better to call than be one of those found dead the next morning.

She remembered how safe she felt staying at Ethel's with Ethel and Miles—and Daisy. She could always do that again or find a room to spend the night. No! She was not going to go crazy, giving into her fear. She was fine. She remembered her mother always told her she had an overactive imagination as a girl. She admitted though, as she pulled in behind her casita, that her mother was never her biggest fan. But she would not think about that now.

She grabbed her purse and her bag of extra scones—"damaged goods are freebies, but don't damage any on purpose, please," her boss Dave had told her, smiling, when he hired her. She had actually left some money with a note this time, so she could treat Ethel to some good ones this morning.

She closed the car door behind her. The snow had stopped falling. She looked around and made a dash for the front door, feeling ridiculous as she did so. Daisy was barking furiously, and Maddy hoped the dog had not awakened Ethel.

What? Daisy ran up to Maddy, then back to the front door, barking. Why was she outside?

"Shhh, Daisy," Maddy whispered. "Do not wake up Ethel."

The dog trotted over, sat next to her, and started whining. Then growling.

The front door was wide open, and Maddy knew she had left it closed, with Daisy inside. She had told Ethel that she could let Daisy out any time, but before dawn? She did not think so. Maddy shivered, and not from the cold.

She tiptoed to the front door, Daisy beside her, and saw splintered wood around the door hinges. She peeked inside and gasped. Chaos. Smithereens of the lovely vase glistened on the floor, slashed couch pillows lay asunder, and from her open bedroom door she could see drawers had been emptied onto the floor. Her fish/bird watercolor was on the floor, one side of the frame smashed. She knew the Flagstaff murderer wielded a knife. Had it been the killer after all, following her from the bakery graveyard shift? She knew late-night workers were his victims. Miles had shared the descriptions of the stabbings. Her heart pulsed so hard inside her chest she was sure an assailant could hear it. She did not want to be the murderer's next victim, but she *was* a late-night worker.

Daisy ran inside, stepping on the glass, and barked excitedly at the closed bathroom door. Fur on her spine stood straight up through her curls.

Maddy ran in and grabbed Daisy's collar, pulling her outside. She turned to Ethel's house, but then hesitated. She would not want to draw a killer to her landlady. She pulled out her cell phone to dial 9-1-1. But before she could dial, she was tackled from behind. The familiar smell of overly sweet aftershave assaulted her nose. No!

Yes!

Arthur stood up, pulling Maddy with him, and raising a baseball bat at Daisy. Before the dog could attack, Arthur hit her. It was the Milwaukee Brewers baseball bat Maddy's brother had given her for a wedding present, the team that they had both loved as kids. She had not gone to any games since Arthur came into her life, she realized now, her brain flipping this way and that in a frenzy of fear and confusion.

"Always the great watch dog," Arthur said, sarcasm dripping from the horrid curl of his lips.

Maddy stood frozen as Arthur wielded the bat over the dog.

"Now you're going to throw down that cell phone, and come inside with me, Maddy. If you do not comply, I will take it out on your precious mutt. You know I will."

Maddy dropped the phone in the dusting of snow and knelt down beside Daisy. She felt the damp soaking into her knees. The dog whined as Maddy ran her hands over the dog's side.

"You have hurt her, Arthur!" Maddy said, incensed. She was *not* going to let this man intimidate her at the expense of her loyal pal. "Now you had better leave us alone or you'll end up in jail."

Arthur yanked her up, jolting her to the reality of his six-foot-plus height and muscular build. She had been drawn to his looks in the early days, but now he repulsed her on every level. Still, she had to keep a clear head, for Daisy. For herself. She shook with fear—and anger. But she realized she needed to play the part of a compliant wife. One more time.

"Please leave her be, Arthur. I will do anything you ask."

"Now that's what I like to hear from my girl," he said, his eyes glistening with—what? Anger, compassion, complete psychosis? *Where was the man I married? Right in front of me*, she realized with a cold clarity.

"If you say you will do anything, then walk yourself back into that shack you live in, and you can pack a bag. Because you are coming home."

Maddy shuddered involuntarily, but if Arthur noticed, he did not say anything.

"I will come inside if you put down that bat," she said, forcing her voice to sound calm, even though her insides felt like jelly. "You are scaring me, Arthur. Truly you are."

"*Truly you are*," he mimicked her. "The first time I heard you say *truly* was at our wedding. When you promised to *truly love me* for better or worse."

He raised the bat higher, and Maddy felt a familiar numbness begin to envelop her. As if she was not standing here, witnessing all of this. It was similar to the many times she had floated out of the room—in her mind—when he took her against her will. The times she ignored her gut instincts that told her he was cheating on her, that he was a liar to the core. She felt like she was watching it all through a distance. *Snap out of it!* She had to come back to reality so she could help her dear Daisy, whose eyes were now closed. Maddy was relieved to see the dog's shallow breaths.

Arthur followed her gaze.

"She is just sleeping, darling," he said, with a smile that appeared authentic. For a moment, Maddy saw the flash of the old Arthur, that man she had fallen for. The charmer who had taken her in, she reminded herself. Except now his hair was disheveled and his eyes were glazed. He looked less put together than she had ever seen him, his white dress shirt untucked. Then he became again who she knew now was the real Arthur, as he grabbed her arm and pulled her into the casita. He was still holding the bat with his other hand. Daisy got up slowly and limped beside her.

Arthur let go of Maddy for just a second and raised the bat toward the dog.

"Arthur, no—"

A loud report exploded, and Maddy saw a circle of red on Arthur's arm right before he dropped the bat. Ethel stood outside the door, an ancient revolver in her steady hands.

He sprang up, holding his wounded arm, and gunfire exploded again, this time missing its mark. Arthur charged the older woman, the force of the contact carrying both of them onto the patio outside. The gun clattered to the ground.

Maddy ran for the weapon, grabbed it, and aimed it at her husband.

"Arthur, let go of Ethel right now. I will shoot, I *truly* will."

Arthur glared straight at Maddy as his fingers encircled Ethel's throat, squeezing.

"Ethel, is it? Or should I say *was* it? This is for you, Maddy," he said, squeezing Ethel's throat.

"Ethel," Maddy screamed.

Ethel's eyes closed, her face turning a pale blue.

Daisy was on her belly, pulling herself toward the pair. Arthur noticed her and pulled back a leg to kick her. But the injured dog was faster than he expected, and she sank her teeth into his leg.

Arthur yelled, dropped Ethel, and ran straight at Maddy.

Who pulled the trigger and watched a new spot of red stain his white shirt. But this spot, a dime-sized circle becoming a silver dollar, was over his heart.

Chapter 49

Maddy cradled Ethel in her one arm as she dialed 9-1-1 with her free hand. Ethel's eyelids opened and closed, but she smiled up at her young friend.

"Got him, did we?" she asked in a frail voice.

"Shhh, just rest now."

"I am fine, dear," Ethel said, a smile still on her lips.

Maddy kept her face turned away from Arthur, who lay motionless three feet away from the women. Daisy lay next to them.

After what seemed like hours but was probably less than three minutes, the sound of a siren and then a car braking came from the street, followed by footsteps.

Luis Ortega and another police officer ran into the yard, weapons drawn.

He quickly took in the scene, walked over to Arthur, and felt for a pulse. He shook his head at the other officer, who was feeling for a pulse on Ethel.

"You all right, Madeline Sullivan?" Ortega asked gently.

"I think so. Can you get her to the hospital?"

Ethel's eyes opened, and this time she smiled up at Ortega.

"I shot him, officer," she said softly.

"I shot him, Detective," Maddy said. "Is he, is he?"

"He is dead. Is this your husband?"

"He was."

Maddy started to shake.

Ortega walked to the other side of the yard and spoke into his radio as the woman officer sat with Maddy and Ethel, rubbing their arms.

Just then, Miles crashed through Ethel's side of the yard.

"Maddy, what's going on?" he asked, catching his breath as he kneeled down beside the women. "Oh my God. Is Ethel dead?"

"Not so fast, boy," Ethel said, her eyes staying closed.

"Find them some blankets, Miles," Ortega ordered.

Miles, who had just left the newsroom after filing the story about the encounter with Harold Boyle, dashed into Ethel's house, as more sirens approached. He came back with an armful of blankets and handed them to the officer on the ground next to the women. Four EMTs came into the small yard. One checked for Arthur's pulse and confirmed Ortega's finding, while another turned his attention to Ethel. After assessing her state, they placed her gently onto a gurney, and two of them carried her off to the ambulance.

Maddy, shaking, started to stand, but sat down suddenly.

"I need to go with Ethel," she said.

"I'll go," Miles said. "I'll be back as soon as she gets settled."

He loped off behind the EMTs.

One of the medics shone a flashlight into Maddy's eyes, took her pulse, and listened to her heart.

"You're going to be fine, miss," she told her. "You've had a shock now, haven't you?"

Maddy nodded.

Another EMT looked over at Ortega and nodded toward Arthur's body.

"I will need to secure the scene first," Ortega said, and then turned back to Maddy.

"They can help you inside, Madeline," he said. "Which house would you like to go to?"

"What about Daisy?" she asked.

Ortega frowned, then understood as she petted the dog's head.

"She seems to be doing all right. I will bring her after we get you inside. Which house?" Ortega asked again.

Maddy looked around. She needed to get as far away as possible from Arthur's body.

"The big house, please."

Ortega nodded to the female medic, who walked Maddy into the house. Ortega leaned down to pick up the dog, who licked his hand, and carried her inside, placing her on the rug near the couch.

He left the room as the EMT settled Maddy in.

Back outside, he pulled out his police radio.

"Got a shooting on Philomena Drive, clean shot, two witnesses," he reported. "Victim dead on the scene."

"10-4. Victim?" crackled the dispatcher's response.

"Arthur Dempster. D-E-M-P-S-T-E-R. Husband of one of the shooters. He was apparently stalking her. From Wisconsin. We have her restraint order on file."

"One of the shooters. How many were there, and was he armed?"

"Still looking at everything. Two shooters. I'd say both those women took a shot at him. We do not know yet which one killed him. Very preliminary findings: He may have been engaged in the act of assaulting one of the women when the other shot him."

"10-4." Pause. "The shooters lovers?"

"Hardly. A landlady in her late seventies, I'd say. And her tenant—the dead man's wife. The EMTs just took the older woman to the ER."

"Jesus. Sounds like a real cluster. Keep me informed."

"10-4. Out."

After the officer took photos and bagged the revolver, Ortega allowed the waiting EMTs to take away the body. He took one more look at the scene and went back inside. Maddy was holding the hand of the EMT, her face looking very relaxed.

"Sleeping meds?" he asked the medic, who nodded.

Miles walked back into the house.

"Back already?" Ortega asked, though he knew the hospital was just a half mile away.

"Ethel's asleep already. And they said she would probably not wake up for at least eight hours," Miles reported. "You okay, Maddy?"

She looked at him with unfocused eyes.

"I will be," she said, her voice slurred. "And Ethel?"

"They said she's going to be fine," Miles answered.

"Daisy?"

Miles knelt down and ran his hand over Daisy's ribs. She licked his fingers now, her tail thumping.

"Pretty sure she's going to be okay, too," Miles said. "Maybe a bruised rib or two. She should see a vet tomorrow."

But Maddy's eyes were closed, her breathing steady.

"She's out," the EMT said. "Are you the boyfriend?"

"Er, no," Miles said, feeling his face flush frustratingly under Ortega's gaze.

"Not by choice," Ortega said quietly, winking at the EMT.

"Well, somebody should stay with her. When she wakes up, she'll have a ton of questions."

"I'll stay for sure. I've got my laptop, so I can work from here."

"I need to talk to Miles for a minute," Ortega said to the medic. "You okay to stay with her for a few more minutes?"

"Of course."

The two men walked out into the yard. It was snowing lightly again and sticking now. Miles could see the now-pink spot in the yard where Arthur Dempster had died. He looked away.

"Listen, Miles, after Madeline filed the order of protection, I read a few reports out of Wisconsin. Arthur Dempster had a clean record, but something felt off. He is—was—a judge, married three times—"

"Wait, what? Maddy was his third wife?"

"That's right. A real Don Juan, looks like. But listen to me. Both his other wives and a few girlfriends had filed DV charges that were later dropped."

"So why do you say he had a clean record?" Miles asked in a low voice, glancing toward Ethel's house.

"That's just it. In my initial search, none of those records showed. When I used my official credentials to get into the national system, they popped right up. So let's just say if somebody, maybe Madeline Sullivan for instance, tried to look up anything on Dempster before—or more likely after—they married? Nothing would have come up in a search by a member of the public."

Miles stared at his friend, letting it all sink in. Ortega continued.

"Dempster was wearing a thousand-dollar suit. His Rolex cost much more than what you and I together make in an entire year," he noted. He opened two sticks of Big Red, folded them into his mouth, and chewed. "That woman of yours walked away from riches most would have swooned over. Hell, I would have."

"Not my woman," Miles said almost out of habit, then dropping his voice to a whisper. "Geez, Luis, that marriage must have been pretty bad."

"Make that very, very bad."

Miles asked Ortega a few formal questions for the newspaper, and the two men parted ways, Miles back into the house and Ortega to his vehicle. Miles went back inside to sit beside Maddy as he tapped a shooting brief on his laptop. Ortega got into his car and turned on the ignition. He let the engine idle for a few minutes though, as his mind went over the scene again. And he reflected on Dempster.

Ortega had not shared with Miles all the details of the of the dead man's files. In a divorce document, one of Dempster's former wives claimed he had choked her into unconsciousness in an erotic act gone wrong. She did not deny that the "sexual asphyxiation" was one of mutual consent. At issue was that when she came to, he was having sex with her previously unconscious body.

She filed for divorce the next day. The file had mysteriously—or perhaps not, given that, as a judge, Dempster was an officer of the court—been sealed closed to the public.

Ortega wondered how many people back in the Midwest would be overjoyed to hear about the death of one bastard named Arthur Dempster. And even though he disapproved of sharing personal opinions over police radio airwaves, his dispatcher had called it right. This was a real cluster. As the *Gazette's* Ruth Swanson would say, a real cluster-fuck.

Chapter 50

It was just two days after the death of Arthur Dempster and the confrontation at the newspaper with Harold Boyle when Miles's phone chirped crickets. He'd changed the ring tone from the Byrds to crickets. He could be the host of Animal Kingdom, he joked to himself, still his best audience. The phone screen read *Luis.*

Miles walked out of Caboose Coffee to answer.

"We got him, Miles," Ortega said.

"Where?"

"The psycho was caught getting off the bus in L.A., a bloody hoodie in his backpack."

"Great, Luis. Want to give me the lowdown over coffee? I'm downtown."

Ten minutes later, a fired-up Ortega walked into the Caboose, shaking snow off his knitted cap with the police insignia. Winter had finally arrived in force, and Flagstaff was glittering under the white on ice. It was an advertisement for a wonderland of winter. He glanced at the map of the world where people stuck brightly colored plastic thumbtacks marking their travels. He tossed his gum into a wastebasket, ordered a black coffee, and joined Miles at a small table. The adjacent tables were empty, the weather so far keeping people at home or out shoveling.

"I cannot believe this cup of mud cost me four

frickin' dollars," Ortega said abruptly.

"Hello to you, too, dude."

"When I was a young cop and went out for coffee with my father and his fellow officers, the whole table would get cups for that price. Got something against Benny's?"

"Their coffee is affordable, right? But undrinkable, in my book. Give me Lacy's or Caboose Coffee any day of the week."

"No wonder you have not been able to buy a house," Ortega shot back. When they were roommates, Ortega had been careful with money compared to Miles, and a couple of times he had helped his friend out with the rent. Miles had always paid him back.

"So whatcha got?" Miles asked.

Ortega glanced around at the empty tables to be sure nobody could hear them. Before he shared details on the California capture, he went over some of what had occurred before Boyle had showed up at the *Gazette* to attack Miles.

"Initially we went after the Arizona Shuttle guy—Stan Trumpet. Could not find him for several days. But the night before Boyle tried to kill you, we located Trumpet. Over in east Texas, where he's from. And we were able to verify that he was in Texas during the time of the carwash murder attempt."

Miles glanced around the quiet shop and pulled out his digital recorder and reporter's notebook. Ortega nodded his consent, and Miles turned on the recorder, holding himself back from peppering his friend with questions. Clearly, Luis wanted to tell it his way.

Ortega took his own smaller notebook out of his shirt pocket and placed it on the table, flipping through it to get to the page he wanted.

"Listen to this. Want to guess what Shuttle Man was doing in the great state of Texas?"

"What?"

"Went all the way over to his hometown in basically bum-fudge Texas to take part in an anti-immigration rally. That was what he had told his boss was 'family business.' "

"Brother."

"We think he may have been responsible for the graffiti you spotted a while back. He'd spent time in jail over in Texas for destruction of property, petty thefts, but never did prison time. No violent crimes against persons."

"Okay."

"So we circled back to Charlie's drug dealer Frank, to teenager Tanak Vohra, to handyman Boyle, and even to Charlie herself. Turns out the drug dealer, who calls himself Frank-man, for God's sake, had been seen by both the Mountain Motel victim Rafat Shukla and Tanak, the victim's cousin. Tanak finally told us about that. He'd talked to the drug dealer about possibly helping him distribute but then got scared. But before that, he had told Frank that he thought his cousin Rafat might know about the dealing. So Tanak was certain that because he had mentioned his cousin to the dealer, the man had been the one who murdered Rafat. He told me he had forgotten about that the first time my team questioned him."

"Wait, what? How would you forget that?" Miles blurted.

"That's what I thought initially. But the kid was so shaken by the murder. Remember he found the body, and it was his cousin after all," Ortega said. He nodded toward the recorder, and Miles placed it on pause and put down his pen. "Turns out, Tanak had other things on his mind as well. He had beaten up one of the high school soccer players because the guy was stalking Tanak's younger sister. He thought he might end up in jail for attacking the other kid. Humiliate his family, all that."

"How bad was the damage to the soccer player?"

"He was bruised, but not seriously. And thank God they went at it via fisticuffs instead of with weapons like so many kids are doing now."

"And adults," Miles mused, and Luis nodded.

"For being the smaller kid, Tanak got in some good punches. I assume he was extra angry because of his kid sister, so that fueled him."

"Why didn't he just tell their parents about his sister, instead of leading everyone on a wild goose chase that pointed to himself as a possible killer?"

"His sister told him about the harassment but would not tell their parents. Classic, she thought it was somehow her fault. She made him promise not to tell their parents. So Tanak decided the only way to help her was to rough up the other kid."

Miles nodded. As he listened, he was happy he could report to Maddy that her instincts about the boy had been right on.

"We also verified that Tanak was not anywhere near the motel the night of the murder. He was out late with friends. He did not want to admit that to his parents. They seem like great people, but fairly protective of their teenagers. He really did just find the body that morning."

Ortega took a sip of his coffee, and Miles did the same.

"Anyway, all that is to say that we eliminated Tanak Vohra. And then Frank-man the drug dealer. We got him on other charges, drug-related. He's in the city/county jail now. The night of the motel attempted murder? He was behind bars."

"Hold on," Miles said. "There was a Frank at the basement meeting I told you about. Skinny as a cactus spine and with creepy eyes?"

"That is the one. So, an anti-immigrant drug dealer," Ortega said, shaking his head.

"And Charlie?"

"Charlotte came to see me and told me everything. Including sharing some incident about her being high and running over a fox and picking up its bloody body up on Snow Bowl Road. Darn confusing and irrelevant, honestly. But she mainly talked about her drug use, her dealing, her getting in way over her head. And then she gave up Frank-man. She took a real risk doing that. She is taking a leave of absence to sort things out, she said."

"Poor Charlie. But good for her. And Beez?"

"He was never really a suspect. Except for in your eyes. For one thing, he does have a back yard full of roses, which matched those scratches that you were all on about. Must be an amazing garden in the summer."

"So all of that put it on Boyle," Miles said.

"It did. Plus, remember the Carruthers woman you interviewed at the protest? She came in to see me at the station the day before Boyle attacked you, said she was frightened out of her wits. She told me about one of Boyle's rants after that protest about 'the dark people,' as he put it. She tried to convince me that while she had a 'dislike' for illegal immigrants, she did not feel that way about all people of color," Ortega recalled. "It was like she wanted me to thank her for that. I had to work to keep my mouth shut. She was nearly too late. Still, her information helped me see Boyle's character more clearly. So I took the high road and thanked her for coming in."

Miles checked to make sure his recorder batteries were still charged and doing their job.

"After Boyle came for you at the paper, he disappeared. We checked the buses. He did not board one in Flagstaff. We think he hitched to Williams, because his ticket stub—which was in the idiot's pocket when they grabbed him in L.A.—showed he boarded there."

"Along with the bloody hoodie," Miles said, shaking his head.

"Along with the bloody hoodie," Ortega said, nodding. "Crazy thing? The L.A. detective told me the blood looked awfully old, so we will have to sort that out. So to tie up everything in a tidy knot—"

"—bow—"

"Knot is more permanent," Ortega argued. "So to tie up everything in a nice knot, Boyle had been hired to clean the windows at the observatory. Also did some odd jobs at—get this—Ethel Naderman's house."

"Oh, Jesus," Miles said, swallowing hard.

"Turns out the guy used to have a cleaning service a decade ago in Flagstaff. He used an alias, which is why he never popped up on our law-enforcement Internet searches. He lost jobs because he started hitting the bottle—hard. Not showing up for work and doing a half-ass job when he did show. So guess who some of his clients were back then."

"The observatory?"

"You guessed it. Plus several motels on Route 66. And the same carwash, back when it had a different name and owner," Ortega said. "When the police officers—one Black, one Hispanic—threw him into a holding cell in southern California, get this. He kept calling them, well, let's just say every derogatory name in the book. He screamed at them that they'd taken away his jobs, stolen his work, ruined his life."

Both men shook their heads and gazed out at the deepening snow on the street.

"Crazies everywhere," Miles said. "Even in Cali."

"Turns out there were a half dozen knifings of undocumented workers in Salinas, where his mother's house is. They are looking into that. The exact same M.O. as ours. Practice killings?"

"Sicko," Miles said. "It's scary that Boyle was right there, watching you arrest the wrong guy at the Milton Road motel. And before that, he walked right into the paper to talk about the observatory killing. I wonder what he was planning on saying to me."

"Possibly to find out how much you knew. He was also hanging around outside the Mountain Motel the morning after he murdered Rafat Shukla. He's one sick bastard. Maybe wanting to be caught. But probably flaunting to himself—or his dead mother—how smart he is."

"Dead mother?"

"Oh, yeah. We reached a counselor over in Salinas, California. Boyle served a couple of years in the California system for having sex with a minor. At the time he was in his thirties and the girl was sixteen.

Swore he did not know, of course. So he was picked up—under a different name. That is why it did not pop up in the sex-offenders registry last month," Ortega said. "Henry Bates is his given name."

"Master Bates," Miles quipped, but his friend ignored him. Miles had not yet told Luis about the note from one Henry Bates.

"So this therapist tells me that Bates/Boyle was trying to get an early release. That is why he agreed to a few counseling sessions. Turns out the guy was obsessed with his mother—to the point that he talked directly to her during his therapy. I mean, as in, the in-his-head mother. The mom was not there. The counselor told me he was upset because his mom never once came to see him inside. She would send him these unbelievable letters calling him all kind of horrible names. Mostly 'Loser. Just like your father, you're a total loser.' Like that. Good old-fashioned familial affection."

"Sheesh. Families," Miles said.

"Now get this. Turns out it looks like our man Harold/Henry may have killed his mother, too. Before he moved on to the other stabbings. California law enforcement is investigating."

Miles just shook his head.

"I called my dad today to talk things through on this case. He reminded me that some of the worst sociopaths had something bad go down when they were kids. Trauma. Said killers come in all stripes, of course. But some of the wackier ones he ran across over the years had strange relationships with at least one of their parents.

"So that is all I have for now," he said. "Oh, except

that Harold/Henry used cash for his bus tickets, so may have gone between California and Arizona multiple times without our knowledge."

The two men finished their drinks.

"How is your Madeline doing?"

"Okay, I guess. Processing a lot of stuff, is how she put it to Ethel, who told me. Can you imagine being married to someone who then tries to kidnap you, and you end up killing him?"

"I would like to say all that is far-fetched. But in my line of business, it is more common than you might think. Domestic abuse is rampant," Ortega said. "How are the two of them doing? Madeline and Ethel?"

"Ethel seems back to her old self, just moving a bit more slowly. But the doctor told her she's coming along great," Miles told him. "Maddy's headed over to New Mexico soon to stay with a childhood friend for a while. You know, to get away from everything."

"Maddy, is it? She your girlfriend yet?"

"No comment," Miles snapped. But his lopsided smile removed the sting.

Ortega reached over and patted Miles on the arm.

"You never had much nerve with the ladies back in the day, either," he teased, shaking his head. "I know somebody who is going to miss the heck out of one Madeline Sullivan while she is gone."

"Yeah, Ethel sure will."

"Now let me give you a piece of advice that Dad gave me way back in high school," Ortega continued. "Make yourself presentable. Women value that."

"Wait, what? How am I not presentable?" Miles asked, sitting taller.

"Maybe if you remove that dead squirrel from your

face. When your Madeline returns to Flagstaff, she will be a bit more attentive."

Miles stroked his chin.

"Abe Lincoln had a beard."

"Oh, so now you're comparing yourself to Honest Abe. You need some therapist to interpret that? Most of you white folks have shrinks, yes? In the meantime, President Lincoln, he had a *beard* beard. A caterpillar has more damn fuzz than you."

Ortega stood.

"Next time, let's not go to a place that charges half a paycheck *para una taza de café*," Ortega said, picking up their ongoing argument.

"I love this coffee. Everybody charges too much."

"Not Miss Sips. Not Martin's. Love their breakfast burritos."

"Those chilaquiles—to die for," Miles agreed. "Let's do Martin's this weekend. No work, just breakfast. Hey, tell your dad to come up."

They shook hands outside and parted ways.

Miles wiped the inch of cold crystals off his savior bike seat with his jacket sleeve, and rode through the falling snow, headed for the newspaper.

Chapter 51

Harold Boyle, aka Master Bates, lay on his jail cot, listening to one more train pass through Flagstaff. During the ten years he lived in Cali, he'd never forgotten the goddamn trains that rattled nonstop through this crappy town, whistles screaming at all hours of the day and night. He'd overheard a couple guards talking about some new city rule that had put a stop to the constant whistles. Couldn't happen a second too soon.

"I hope I made ya proud, Mother," he whispered into the pre-dawn darkness. Well, he could tell it was dark outside, but the goddamn lights were on all night here. "I got rid of those foreigners, and the jobs they had will be filled again with our own kind. Too bad I was caught, or I'd be starting back up my cleaning business."

It wouldn't be that bad going back inside. Three squares and no need of a job. He wasn't looking forward to living amongst all those different colored men, but guys pretty much kept to their own kind in prison.

He still resented having served time for some trumped-up sexual charges that some little bitch made up. How was he supposed to know she was barely sixteen? Well, she hadn't fought much—after he plied her with cranberry juice and vodka. Hell, she looked at least twenty-five to his thirty. *Hello! Had nobody heard of first offenses, for God's sake*?

He'd resolved in prison that he'd never touch another woman and never drink another drop. It hadn't been that tough. Most women were liars and whores, and his mind was more focused without the fog of booze. His clear mind had helped him hatch his plot for revenge.

Before he got into trouble, he had a respected cleaning business, even regular clients. Nobody seemed to *like* him all that much, but that was mutual. Still, he did the job well. Until he started hitting the bottle, missing deadlines, fucking up in general—even on getting the goddamn places *cleaned.* One by one he lost his jobs, his clients, and he knew he had to get out. He'd stupidly stolen from the gas station/carwash and vandalized the motel. He was caught and given a date to report to court.

That's when he'd left for California and changed his name to Harold Boyle (his given "Henry Bates" long forgotten with the rest of his rotten childhood years). Much later, he made his plans to come back and take Flagstaff by storm.

He thought about the drunk at the motel. The stupid boozer had easily fallen for his story about needing to be on the first floor 'cause of a fear of heights. And the forty bucks he'd slipped Rheumy Eyes had clinched the deal. *Almost too easy a target.*

When Boyle stood behind the sawhorses between the motel and the carwash across the street from the college and watched the cops pull the drunk out of his former room, he'd felt the thrill. Of defying law enforcement, the Authority, the Man. Especially when he noted that the cop who seemed to be in charge was a Mexican, for Christ's sake.

His first time back to Flagstaff had been a scouting trip. He'd visited all the places he'd worked back then. He'd planned to get a contract to clean at the observatory and the carwash, and the motels along Route 66—though the historic road had changed and only a couple of the motels were still there. To be a picture of a good citizen, he'd even done some odd jobs for an old lady up in the hospital neighborhood. Washing windows, pulling weeds. And even got hired to wash windows up on the observatory on Mars Hill again. At his former places of work, he'd seen with his own eyes that he'd been replaced with non-Americans. He knew he had to make room for himself, somehow. Then, he paid a visit to the observatory late one night.

He thought of the woman inside the observation calling out something in Spanish, right before she died. After he'd stabbed her, he'd hightailed it back to Salinas. He wanted to get out of town while things cooled off. Plus, he had stuff to wrap up in the Golden State. He'd closed up his mother's house—no, his house now—and hopped back on the Greyhound. It was always good to have a plan.

Now he stretched his arms over his head, smirking to himself as he remembered the young man at the motel, singing some fucking Paki or Iraqi song. Boyle had made the world a better place without *that* voice.

And then there was the long-haired Indian at the carwash. The kid was keeping an eye on him as if the punk had more of a right to be here than Boyle did, for God's sake. The kid had been giving him the evil eye every time Boyle walked in from the motel to grab a cola at the carwash/gas station. Boyle was disgusted when it hit him that there wasn't even *one* white guy working there anymore. It had been more than a decade that he'd done the cleaning for the then-smaller place. Back then the owner had been white but must have sold out to some dark-skins and moved on. Whoever owned it now hired more of their kind—the "minorities" as the Lefties called them.

He rolled over to his side and heard the bunk squeak under his weight. Damn. He was in this jail cell instead of Rheumy. After his arrest in California, he had been transported back to Flagstaff in an eighteen-passenger state van.

Well, at least he'd gotten rid of a few more of those "minorities." Several, if he counted the illegals he'd knifed in the hell hole Salinas—for practice. Too bad he hadn't been able to off that stupid newsman when he had the chance. But he was damn proud of how he ditched the newspaper office and then the coppers that night. *Disappearing into the night like that is a skill*!

The fact that his mother had moved to Salinas when he was doing time for those years just about killed him. Smack between yuppie towns like Santa Cruz and Monterey, Salinas was chock full of illegals who were stealing jobs from hard-working American men like himself. It was sickening to get out of the joint, only to move to his mother's and find she had befriended her neighbors. Trading her vegetables for eggs or goat's milk.

Anymore, non-Americans got the first shot at everything. And now a damn African in the White House? Unfuckingbelievable!

Because he'd been arrested now and would

certainly go back to prison—maybe for the rest of his life—he'd not been able to get his cleaning job back. Obviously. But instead of the cleaning job, he'd done a *cleansing* job.

"Get it, Mother? Flagstaff cleansing. Hahaha."

No answer. Sometimes she went all quiet on him.

Not the night she died, though, in her little Salinas shack.

He'd held her in his arms as she faded away. She couldn't believe she was dying.

"Why?" she had whispered, her eyes beginning to glass over.

"Why not?" he answered her, blood soaking both of their clothes.

Stabbing someone was a lot messier than he'd thought. That was his first time, his virgin kill, as he came to think of it. He'd cleaned up all the blood and kissed her forehead before folding her body into a large black plastic bag, from the ones she normally used for grass clippings and leaves.

"Goodbye, Mother. Sorry I was never perfect enough for you."

After changing his bloody clothes, he put them into the bag, and tossed it into an alley dumpster the night before garbage pickup day. He was surprised at the lightness of someone who, at five foot three inches tall, always seemed bigger than life. At the last moment, he'd decided to keep the bloody hoodie he'd been wearing when he held her. He would keep it at the bottom of his backpack, to remind himself she was really gone from his life. He bought three more hoodies before returning to Flagstaff. Red, white, and blue. His patriotism out there for all to see.

At first, he felt lighter after Mother was gone. No more hearing about what a disappointment he was, how he would never compare to his father—who had deserted the two of them when Harold, or actually Henry, was just a boy, leaving him as the person she leaned on in her drunken, violent sprees.

Still, after time, he was surprised that he missed her voice. Soon, though, he realized he could bring her back—in his mind.

Now Boyle heard a jail door being unlocked, and the sound of heavy footsteps approaching. He wondered what the Coconino County jail served for breakfast. His mouth watered, and he realized how hungry he was. Starving, actually.

A guard stood outside his cell, staring at Boyle. He was giant-tall, grim-faced, with black hair pulled back into a ponytail. Just his luck. No breakfast tray either.

He lay back down on his cot, face to the wall.

"Yo, that's right. Turn away, man," hissed the Native American guard. "Like my cousin tried to turn away from you at the carwash. That was my baby cousin, all set to *try* a new chapter in his life."

Boyle let that sink in. He'd said "was." Okay, he'd killed one more. The pride filled him like the warm glow of a campfire.

"I'll be back this morning to *try* giving you safe passage to your initial court appearance," the guard said. "*Try* my very best."

Then the footsteps receded, and the door clicked shut.

"How good is that, Mother?" he whispered into the stale air of the cell. "One more for my list."

Still, his lips felt dry, and he found it hard to

swallow.

Let's see you get out of this one, you stupid boy, Mother sneered.

Harold covered his head with his hard, jail-issued pillow.

Stupid, stupid boy.

Chapter 52

Miles and Maddy held hands. They stood side by side on her tiny front porch, watching the evening snowfall.

Maddy felt her heart skip. Was she happy? Was she scared? What?

An image of Arthur's body, blood soaking his shirt, flashed in her head. She forced it away.

If Miles took her wrists, the way Arthur used to before he started to hit her, and much more, she knew she could not do this. *Do what?* she wondered.

But Miles's fingers were long and warm and held hers gently, the only pressure a light squeeze of affection.

"How ya doin', Maddy Sullivan?" he asked quietly.

It was a week after the Big Night, as the two of them and Ethel referred to the night Arthur was killed and Miles nearly murdered. Maddy and Miles had spent a lot of time together since. But this was the first time he'd found the nerve to take her hands, and he felt his heart pounding as loud as one of the gazillion trains rushing through town.

She squeezed back, and then freed her hands and looked at him. His smile, lopsided as usual, was warm and open. Just like him.

"To tell you the truth? Overwhelmed still," she

said, crossing her arms. "I am still trying to get over the reality that I killed my husband. And that I was even married to such a man."

"Don't forget that Ethel also shot him, Maddy. You two were protecting each other."

"I know," she said, her voice irritated. She took a big breath. "But there's still this strange, I guess, regret. Not about Arthur being gone from my life forever. But, first, that I was so blind about him that I married him. And, second, that I was so numb that I stayed with him for three whole years. But, even more, that I was capable of killing someone. I cannot get that night out of my head. I see it all over again when I close my eyes at night."

"I'm sure."

They were both quiet for a few minutes.

"I have cried my eyes out nearly every night this week, honestly. Poor Daisy has had her fur soaked over and over again," she said, leaning down to pat her pal. "Look, I am seriously exhausted. I am going to go inside. But, Miles, I want to thank you for everything you have done for me. I mean, even before all this, this, well, you know. The way you welcomed me to town, took me—and Daisy—on those hikes, met us for coffee. All of that."

Miles fought his disappointment, quite valiantly, he reflected later.

"Sounds like a goodbye, a let's-just-be-friends speech," he said quietly.

She reached over, took his face in her hands, and drew him in for a kiss. A real kiss.

When they finally pulled apart, his face nearly split apart in that grin of his.

"Oh," he said.

"Mmm," she answered, surprised as well. She stepped away. "Remember I head out tomorrow for New Mexico to be with Belinda. It will be so nice to be with an old friend for the holidays. We have so much to talk about. I have never met her partner. Not sure what I will do in the long run."

"Right," Miles said, trying to think beyond the kiss. The amazing kiss. "Take your time, Maddy. Deciding, well, everything. But know I'll be here for you if and when you come back. I sure hope you do."

"I am going to get some counseling, figure out the whole marriage disaster—on so many levels—and also consider what I will do with my career."

"Listen," Miles said, a smile playing on his lips. "I've read about sex therapy. If a counselor recommends wonderful sex to help you, you know, recover, I am here to volunteer in any way possible."

"I will surely remember that, Romeo."

He leaned in hesitantly, and they kissed again, a gentle one this time.

"Okay," she said. "I really have to go. It is freezing out here."

"You take care of yourself. Text me when you're there safe and sound, will you?"

"Yes, Daddy," she teased. "Oh, wait. I have been meaning to ask you. How is the carwash kid?"

"Healing really well. One of his sisters who lives in Los Angeles came over. Once he's back on his feet, he's moving out there with her," Miles said. "Apparently that was the plan all along. He was saving up for the move. Cool thing? The owner of the carwash gave him five grand to help with anything he needed.

She was so grateful that Freddie was okay. Told me in an interview that customers had told her after the incident her how well he'd always treated everybody. He's ready for his new life with family in California."

"Wonderful," Maddy said, though knowing the young man would live with the trauma for a long time.

Miles wanted to lean in for Kiss Number 3, but a noble guy or a fool, he resisted. He leaned down to give Daisy a pat and walked backward off the porch steps.

"Oh, one more question, Miles?"

He turned and looked back at her through the light snow. Was she going to ask him to spend the night? A guy could dream.

"Yes?"

"Why did you shave?"

He stroked his smooth cheeks and chin.

"My boss told me it looked like a rodent had died on my face. Luis, too. Also, when he showed me the jail intake photos of the killer, I decided I just didn't want to look seedy anymore."

"Well, it suits you, the clean-shaven look."

"Glad you approve," he said. He swore *not* to tell Luis that his friend had been right about Miles's look, at least when it came to one woman.

He cleared the snow off his bike, waved, and headed down the hill.

Daisy followed him to end the of the driveway and stood looking after him, tail wagging back and forth, until the bike light was out of sight. She trotted back onto the porch, where dog and human both watched the road for another full minute. Then they left the cold night air behind, the dog shaking off the melting snow. They walked into the warmth and light of the casita.

Chapter 53

Miles flipped and flopped most of the night, catching only snatches of sleep. His mind raced, feeling Maddy's lips on his, wondering if he'd ever feel them again. He finally rolled out of bed around five.

He switched out the regular mountain bike tires to a pair of thicker winter treads—about time—working quickly. He fantasized about checking out used cars or trucks one of these days, for crying out loud. But as he looked at both his bikes, one orange, one green, and thought about how this one had probably saved his life, he shoved the real-deal vehicle thought away. His bicycles were extensions of himself. Kind of like Daisy was part of Maddy. Plus, he didn't need to feed them gas every few weeks. Then again, lots of people were jumping in on the new trend of electric bikes these days. Most people using them were his mom's age, but still. It would be a compromise. Or *could* be. For now, though, it was the mountain bike on fat tires.

He splashed ice-cold water on his face, feeling its intensity without the layer of dead squirrel. He looked in the mirror. Okay, they'd been right, damnitall. He did look ten times better without the damn critter. His hazel eyes looked bigger sans fuzzy caterpillar. And he looked much younger. Funny, for most of his life he longed to look older than his years. Now he finally liked looking younger. What was with that?

He made a cup of coffee, fried two eggs over easy, and toasted two slices of sourdough rye, slathering them with butter and raspberry jam. He ate while reading Hillerman's *The Shape Shifter.* It was the last mystery novel Tony Hillerman wrote before he died in 2008. Miles remembered being devastated by the news of the author's death, as if he'd lost a lifelong friend. Miles had started reading the novel three months ago, but it had waited on his bedside table since the first of the Flagstaff murders. This was the only time he'd not read a Hillerman cover to cover in a couple, few days. The real-life drama in Flag had kept him from the fiction. It felt good to get back to the fictional mystery.

As he ate his early breakfast, he re-introduced himself to the characters of Joe Leaphorn, Jim Chee, and Bernadette Manuelito. In many of Hillerman's mysteries, Navajo characters came to life as the books examined how peoples' choices might impact their dreams.

He rested the book on the kitchen table, letting his mind drift. He thought about the dreams of Alejandra Lopez and Rafat Shukla, who would never see them come to be. He thought about the Dreamers, who were real and dreamed of a better life in the United States. And of the mostly white men who were afraid of all that—like Stan Trumpet, Frank-man, and of course Harold Boyle/Henry Bates.

Miles stood and stretched, chewing a bite of toast and absently looking around for Daisy to gulp down the last of the crusts. He already missed her fuzzy, happy spirit. He knew she was pulling for him.

He wondered how Charlie was doing in rehab, how Freddie Begay Junior was recovering, and how the two families of the murder victims were holding up. He'd do a follow-up story this week about all of them. And then tweet it all into the atmosphere, as his job demanded.

He turned his thoughts to what else his workday might bring. Probably nothing quite as exciting as the Hillerman mysteries, or in fact the recent events of real-life Flagstaff. But Miles knew a reporter's job included the mundane, the routine, the regular people, as well as the extremes. And that was just fine with him.

Today he had a meeting at work about the new deadlines, what with the *Gazette* becoming a morning paper. Ruth had told him there would be discussions on blogging and the paper's Facebook and Instagram pages, and how everyone must have a Twitter work account by New Year's Day. Finally, his newspaper would be catching up with the journalism trends that were now commonplace with most other media.

Still, the evolving technology didn't mean reporters couldn't write in-depth, insightful stories. He clicked on his bike helmet and wheeled his bike out the door, holding it up so just the back wheel hit the floor until he was outside.

He rode toward the paper, noting the cool air and the lack of falling snow. He wanted to find an angle for a story about the racism that was creeping significantly into this town, the Southwest, the country. How to do it without revealing his own biases?

And he had dinner plans with Ethel. And maybe he'd ask his mom to come to Flag for the holidays.

And then there was Maddy. It would be way different with her out of town. Funny how he'd gotten used to having her around when she'd only arrived in

Flagstaff, what, three months ago? He wondered if she'd call or text him right when she got back. *God, let her come back*, he thought. He shoved that aside. *No, let her do what's best for her*, his better self corrected. Though, honestly, he didn't feel that way.

The crickets chirped from his belt. Was she calling already?

Caller I.D. denied him.

"What's up?" he answered, slowing down.

"Got another big one, Miles," Ruth barked. "A fuckin' story with your name on it. Roll out of that nice warm bed and get over here—pronto."

"I'm halfway there already," he said.

Typical of Ruthless, she'd already hung up.

He pedaled harder, speeding to the newspaper he loved, the chilly air stinging his naked face. His phone chirped again. Miles grinned and kept on riding.

A word about the author…

Award-winning journalist Mary Tolan has reported on education, gun violence, and community news in the Southwest for four decades. For twenty years she taught journalism at Northern Arizona University in Flagstaff. Between reporting and teaching, she snuck in time for her passion: fiction writing.

The third of six children, Tolan grew up in Wisconsin, and lives in Flagstaff. Her awesome children are grown.

She and her dog Maxx run and hike on northern Arizona forest trails, where she imagines the next fictional crime scene. Mars Hill Murder is her first published novel.

Thank you for purchasing
this publication of The Wild Rose Press, Inc.

For questions or more information
contact us at
info@thewildrosepress.com.

The Wild Rose Press, Inc.
www.thewildrosepress.com